THE WITCH TREE SYMBOL

When a neighbor asks Nancy Drew to accompany her to an old uninhabited mansion, a new mystery opens up, and danger lurks on the second floor. Nancy finds a witch tree symbol that leads her to Pennsylvania Dutch country in pursuit of a cunning and ruthless thief.

The friendly welcome the young detective and her friends Bess and George receive from the Amish people soon changes to hostility when it is rumored that Nancy is a witch! Superstition helps her adversary in his attempt to get her off his trail, but Nancy does not give up. Persistently she uncovers one clue after another.

Nancy's intelligence and sleuthing ability finally lead to the fascinating solution of this puzzling case.

The bull lowered his head to make another attack!

NANCY DREW MYSTERY STORIES®

The Witch Tree Symbol

BY CAROLYN KEENE

GROSSET & DUNLAP
Publishers • New York
A member of The Putnam & Grosset Group

Contents

The Witch Tree Symbol

CHAPTER I

A Mysterious Intruder

"I wouldn't go into that spooky old house alone for anything," declared the plump, nervous woman who sat beside Nancy Drew in her convertible.

Nancy, a slender, attractive girl of eighteen, smiled as she turned the car into the winding, tree-shaded drive of the Follett mansion. "Why, Mrs. Tenney," she said, "your great-aunt lived here alone for many years and was safe."

"She was just lucky not to have had burglars," Mrs. Tenney replied. "Aunt Sara was so absent-minded that most of the time she didn't know what was going on. But one thing she did keep track of was the beautiful antique furniture in her library. She never used the room, but wouldn't part with any of its contents."

As Nancy parked the car in front of the faded

green Victorian house, she remarked, "Everything looks peaceful. Shall we go in?"

Mrs. Tenney gazed askance at the closed draperies, then said, "I suppose we must. After all, that's why I asked you to come. Oh, Nancy, wait until you see the furniture. Especially the two matching cherry tables George Washington once used. They're priceless. And to think that I've inherited half of everything in this house!"

Nancy and her companion alighted. Mrs. Tenney unlocked the front door. Snapping on a light, she led the way to a large hall, on each side of which were arched entrances to various rooms. Nancy followed her to an archway on the right that lead to the library. Mrs. Tenney stopped abruptly and gasped.

"What's the matter?" Nancy asked.

"They're gone! All the valuable antiques!" the woman cried out. Frantically she hurried into the library, paused, and pointed. "There's where a fine old sofa stood. At each end was one of the tables I told you about."

Mrs. Tenney wept. Then, as a sudden thought struck her, she stopped and said, "Well, he won't get away with this!"

The blond-haired, blue-eyed girl waited for the woman to explain her statement. Nancy had met Mrs. Tenney only a short time ago and felt it would be presumptuous to question her at the moment. The woman had recently moved into Nancy's neighborhood. Having heard that the young detective was courageous and level-headed, she had asked Nancy to accompany her to the dreary Follett mansion. She did not want to be alone in the house while she took inventory of the furnishings recently willed to her.

"My second cousin!" she burst out. "Alpha Zinn! He came here and took the best pieces before I had a chance to decide on what I wanted!"

Nancy ventured a question. "Was Mr. Zinn bequeathed the other half of the contents of this house?"

"Yes. We have never been friends. I don't trust him. He's an antique dealer and a sharp trader."

Nancy did not feel that these were valid reasons for the woman's accusations, especially when half the furniture belonged to Zinn, anyway. "Perhaps it was someone else," the detective suggested. "Let's look for a clue to the burglar."

Even though all the furniture had been moved out of the library, there were bookcases that had been built into the walls, radiator covers, and wastebaskets standing about. A few books remained on the shelves, but other than that there was little evidence of anything else having been left behind.

Nancy began searching carefully. In a corner of the library she picked up a small, crumpled piece of paper. Drawn on it in colored crayon was a white-rimmed circle with a red center in which was a black star. Printed underneath the circle were the words: WITCH TREE SYMBOL.

"How very strange!" Nancy thought, as she showed it to Mrs. Tenney. "Do you know what this is?" she asked.

The woman gave the drawing one glance, then said, "Of course. It's a Pennsylvania Dutch hex sign. Well, I guess that's all the proof we need," she stated flatly. "Alpha Zinn lives in that part of Pennsylvania. I just know he was here and took every stick of good furniture. Not only his, but mine!"

Nancy had to admit that under the circumstances Mr. Zinn was a logical suspect, but she was not convinced of his guilt. "What does 'witch tree symbol' mean?" she asked.

"I don't know," Mrs. Tenney replied. "But what difference does that make when I know Alpha is guilty?"

Although Nancy felt sure that the hex sign might be the clue to solving the mystery she did not say so. Whether Mrs. Tenney's cousin or someone else were the real culprit, he very likely had come from the area where quaint hex designs, originated in the days of witchcraft, are sometimes painted on barns. Nancy questioned Mrs. Tenney further about the hex sign. But the woman could throw no light on the strange symbol's significance.

"Do you know what this is?" Nancy asked.

"When were you in this house last?" Nancy asked.

"About a week ago. I came here with one of the executors," Mrs. Tenney explained. "He gave me a key and said I might come back any time I wished."

Mrs. Tenney went on to say that the executor had left and she had stayed behind to inspect some of the furnishings upstairs. But she had begun to feel uneasy alone in the old mansion and had decided to leave.

"Are you sure you locked the front door?" Nancy asked.

Mrs. Tenney thought for a few moments. She frowned and then said, "I'm sure that man locked the door after us."

"What man?" Nancy inquired. "I thought you said the executor had already left."

"Oh, it wasn't the executor," Mrs. Tenney answered quickly. "It was the antique dealer."

Nancy sighed. The woman certainly was giving a confused account of things! But she patiently urged Mrs. Tenney to tell the whole story.

"Well, this is the way it happened that day," the woman confided. "I was just going to lock the door when a nice-looking man drove up. He said that he had heard about Mrs. Follett's collection. He was interested in buying any articles that her heirs did not want, so I took him into the library for a quick look. When we came out I gave him the key to lock the door."

"I see," Nancy said, thinking how easy it would have been for the man to pretend to lock it. "Please go on."

"The man said he had read about Aunt Sara's antiques in a newspaper. He was in River Heights on business and decided to drive over here to look at the pieces."

"Then he wasn't a local dealer," Nancy commented thoughtfully. "Where did this man come from?"

"I don't know." Mrs. Tenney shrugged. "But he was staying at a hotel in town."

Nancy pondered this information for a full minute. Then she said there was a good possibility this man might be the furniture thief and should be investigated at once.

"At which hotel was he staying?" she asked.

Mrs. Tenney flushed with embarrassment, admitting that she could not remember, nor could she recall his name.

"It doesn't matter," said Nancy. "We can go to each hotel in town and inquire about guests interested in antique furniture."

As Nancy finished speaking, she and Mrs. Tenney became aware of light footsteps overhead. Someone was on the second floor! Mrs. Tenney stood frozen to the spot, every bit of color drained from her face. But without a moment's hesitation Nancy dashed to the stairway.

"Oh, don't go up there!" Mrs. Tenney gasped, "You might get hurt!"

Nancy stopped, not because of the warning, but because she heard stairs creaking. The intruder was probably trying to escape!

"Is there a back staircase?" Nancy asked Mrs. Tenney. As she received no answer, she whirled around.

To her dismay, Mrs. Tenney lay on the floor in a faint. Although Nancy realized that the intruder might escape, she rushed to give the woman first aid. A few moments later Mrs. Tenney's eyelids flickered open. Instantly Nancy dashed off in pursuit of the intruder.

But the pause had proved to be costly. When she reached the back of the old mansion, Nancy found the outside kitchen door open. Looking out, she saw a tall, slender man disappearing through a hedge at the rear of the property.

Nancy felt it would be useless to try to overtake him. She locked the back door and returned to Mrs. Tenney. The woman was sitting on the staircase.

"How do you feel?" Nancy asked.

"Oh terrible, just terrible." Mrs. Tenney moaned. "Please drive me home."

"Right away." Nancy locked the front door and

helped the woman into the car. On the way to Mrs. Tenney's house, Nancy asked for a full description of the antique dealer. Although the woman was almost too distraught to talk, Nancy learned that he was tall, slender, and dark, with flashing eyes, and was soft-spoken.

"But I'm sure he's not the thief," Mrs. Tenney insisted, as Nancy pulled up in front of her home. "I still think that cousin of mine is responsible. Aunt Sara always said he kept an eagle eye on her antiques. Of course, I'd hate to have him aware that I'm suspicious of him. But I'd certainly like to know if I'm right."

Then, as a sudden thought struck Mrs. Tenney, she added, "Nancy, would you like to take this case for me? Please. You're a good detective. Go see Alpha Zinn and find out whether he took the antiques."

Nancy promised she would think it over and let the woman know. Right now, she would drive downtown to find out about the mysterious antique dealer who was staying in River Heights.

"By the way," Nancy asked, "what does your cousin look like?"

"Oh, he's short and plump," Mrs. Tenney replied. "He eats too much."

Mrs. Tenney got out of the car and Nancy hurried off on her search. She went from hotel to hotel. As she did, she told herself that if her hunch was right, the suspect would have had plenty of time to check out and escape.

Finally at the Pickwick Arms, she repeated her query: Was a tall, slender, dark-haired, soft-spoken man registered there? Nancy added that she did not know his name, but wanted to get in touch with him about some antique furniture he had examined.

The clerk smiled and said, "I guess you mean Mr. Roger Hoelt. I'm sorry, miss, but you're too late. He rushed in here, packed in a hurry, and checked out about fifteen minutes ago!"

CHAPTER II

Sleuthing Plans

"DID Mr. Hoelt leave a forwarding address?" Nancy asked the hotel clerk.

"No," the man replied, "but you might find him listed in the New York City telephone directory. He gave that as his business address."

Nancy was disappointed. She had been certain that the antique dealer had dropped the paper with the hex symbol, and had therefore come from Pennsylvania Dutch country!

Another idea occurred to her. Nancy identified herself and said that Mr. Hoelt was a suspect in a questionable business deal.

"Perhaps some of your records can help me locate him," the girl said. "Did he make any long-distance telephone calls?"

"I'll look up his bill," the clerk offered and went into his office. In a short time he returned and said, "Mr. Hoelt phoned Lancaster, Pennsylvania, three days ago. He talked a long time, according to the charges."

Nancy's heart was beating fast. Lancaster *was* in Pennsylvania Dutch country! "Have you a record of the number?" she inquired.

"The operator told me the call was to a pay station," the clerk replied. "I can give you the number, but I'm afraid it won't help."

Nancy thanked the man and left the Pickwick Arms. Her eyes were glowing. She was never happier than when working on a mystery. From the time her father had asked her to help him solve *The Secret of the Old Clock* to the recent hazardous *The Scarlet Slipper Mystery*, the young detective never let a suspect elude her for long.

Now, as she thought about Roger Hoelt, Nancy was more convinced than ever that he had stolen the valuable antiques from the Follett mansion a day or two earlier. Perhaps he had called a friend in Pennsylvania to pick up the furniture in a truck.

"Hoelt may be listed in the police files," Nancy mused. "I'll ask Chief McGinnis."

The River Heights police captain, an old friend of Nancy's, greeted her warmly as she entered his office. "Well, Nancy!" He grinned. "Have you found a new mystery already?"

"Now stop teasing," Nancy said. "Yes, I am working on another case. I need some information about Roger Hoelt. He may live in New York City."

Chief McGinnis went to a filing cabinet. He riffled quickly through a series of cards.

"Here it is," he said. "Roger Hoelt, six feet, slender, dark. Eyes, brown; nose, pointed; slight scar on tip of chin; soft-spoken; married. Lived as a child in Lancaster, Pennsylvania. Well, young lady, is that your man?"

"That sounds like him."

The chief told Nancy that Hoelt was a jewel thief who had served a prison term for holding up jewelry stores. "Made one big haul right here in River Heights," he said, handing Nancy the man's picture. "But he's out free now," he added.

After studying the photograph, Nancy informed the chief that she suspected Hoelt of stealing some antique furniture from the Follett mansion. "Has Mrs. Tenney reported it missing?"

"No."

Nancy telephoned Mrs. Tenney and the woman spoke with the police chief. He promised to send two men to investigate the Follett house, and advised Mrs. Tenney to notify the executors immediately.

"I want a complete list of the missing articles," he directed.

When the chief had completed his conversation, Nancy said she hoped to arrange a trip to

Lancaster, Pennsylvania, to search for Hoelt and the missing furniture.

"Maybe you'll find the thief before we do!" Chief McGinnis predicted, bidding her good-by.

At home, Nancy was greeted by her tall, handsome father, a well-known attorney, and Hannah Gruen, the motherly housekeeper who had lived with the family since Mrs. Drew's death many years before.

"Nancy," Hannah said, "don't you ever get hungry? We've waited dinner an hour for you."

Nancy apologized and during the meal described the mystery that had delayed her.

"Mrs. Tenney wants me to go to Pennsylvania Dutch country and prove that her cousin is the one who removed the antiques from the Follett home," she said. "I'd like to make the trip, even though I'm convinced the real thief is Roger Hoelt."

From her purse, Nancy took the paper bearing the strange hex symbol. "I'm sure this is a good clue," she told her father and Hannah. "The prowler at the mansion today might have been Hoelt. He probably returned to get this, but I picked it up first."

Carson Drew agreed that a trip to the Pennsylvania Dutch area probably would be fruitful. It might also be dangerous. He suggested that Nancy ask her friends Bess and George to join her.

"A great idea!" Nancy exclaimed enthusiastically. "I'll call them right away!"

Bess and George, who were cousins, were eager to make the trip and soon received their parents' permission. When the plans were settled, Nancy helped Hannah with the dishes.

"Where's Togo?" she asked, missing her frisky terrier, usually underfoot at dinnertime.

"Oh, I let him out for a run just before you came home," Hannah replied. "But you'd better see what's happened to him."

Nancy went to the backyard and whistled. When the dog did not respond, she began to worry. She walked to the front of the house and whistled.

As she waited, she observed a car that had driven slowly by the Drews' home was not turning the corner. Instead, the driver made a U-turn and the vehicle came back down the street.

At this moment, there was a joyous bark, and Togo raced from the backyard of the house opposite Nancy's. Eager to greet his young mistress, the little dog dashed across the street.

"Oh!" Nancy gasped, as the driver of the car, almost upon the dog, put on a burst of speed, and headed directly for Togo.

Before Nancy could act, the car hit the terrier and the dog gave a yelp of pain!

"Togo!" Nancy cried, running to her pet as

the car flashed past. The animal was whining and yelping pitifully. Nancy feared that he had been seriously injured.

Leaning over to examine the dog, she noticed a long cut on his hip, but there were no other marks. Just then Togo stood up, shook himself and licked her hand. The beloved pet would be all right!

Nancy carried the dog inside and bathed his cut with antiseptic. "That driver deliberately tried to kill Togo!" she told Hannah. "I was so frightened that I forgot to look at him or his license number."

Hannah frowned. "Nancy, perhaps that hex symbol means business," she declared.

"Oh, Hannah, people today don't believe in hexes or witches or spells." Nancy smiled. "And the hex signs that were once used to ward off witches are now decorations on barns and other places. Some people even use them inside their homes."

"Maybe, but I think you should give up the trip," Hannah persisted. "Let the police worry about the robbery. You stay home."

"Why, Hannah, I couldn't do that when I've promised to help Mrs. Tenney," Nancy protested. "Besides, I want a chance to practice my German in Pennsylvania Dutch country!" She smiled.

Mr. Drew, who had been talking on the second-floor telephone, now joined them. He was relieved to learn that Togo was all right.

Hannah told him she was worried about Nancy, but the lawyer did not share her point of view.

"As to the hex business, we are intelligent people and don't believe in witchcraft. If Nancy is careful, I think it will be safe for her to make the trip."

The young detective was preparing to leave the next morning when a special delivery letter arrived for her.

"Trouble," Hannah Gruen predicted gloomily.

The envelope was postmarked Montville, a town about twenty miles from River Heights. Nancy quickly tore open the envelope and pulled out a single sheet of paper. On it was the strange hex symbol. Underneath the witch tree was a boldly printed warning: STAY HOME!

CHAPTER III

Chust for Pretty

NANCY was excited but not alarmed. If the letter was from the thief, he knew she was going to Pennsylvania Dutch country. Montville was en route to Lancaster. She hoped this meant that she had correctly figured his destination.

"I'm not frightened by this note," Nancy said when Hannah again urged her to stay home. She kissed the housekeeper good-by and drove off in her convertible.

In a few minutes she reached the home of pretty, blond, blue-eyed Bess Marvin. She was eager to begin the trip.

"Pennsylvania Dutch cooking is famous!" she exclaimed. "What meals we'll have!"

Trim, dark-haired George Fayne, who lived nearby, climbed into the car soon afterward. "Grand day, isn't it?" she said with gusto. "August weather's great for a vacation."

"And perfect weather for solving a mystery." Nancy laughed.

"Tell us about it," Bess begged. "I hope it's not a dangerous one," she added.

As they rode along, Nancy told the story. Bess became concerned. She shivered when she heard of the hex symbol. "Do you believe in it?" she asked.

Nancy assured her she did not. "But," she declared, "I understand there are some people in the back country of Pennsylvania who still think it's possible to hex people."

Several hours later, the girls began to notice hex signs on the barns they passed. Even Bess had to admit that the various circular designs, using birds, stars, and crosses, were very colorful and attractive. Seeing a farmer coming from a large red barn, Nancy stopped the car. After chatting a moment, she asked him about the designs' true significance.

The burly man smiled and replied, "It's *chust* for pretty."

"It's not part of a superstition?" Bess asked.

The man shook his head. "No. *Chust* to make pretty the barn. But some folks think it is to chase witches. That is foolish, ain't?"

The girls nodded, thanked him, and drove on.

George laughed. "He had a quaint way of speaking. We may have some trouble understanding what people say in these parts."

Nancy agreed. "And if we don't understand, I think we'd better tell the speaker."

As the girls rode through methodically planned, beautiful farm country, they saw straight green fields of corn, as well as potatoes and tobacco. Weedless vegetable gardens were surrounded by neat borders of flowers—cockscomb, begonia, and geranium bloomed in profusion.

"Where is Mr. Alpha Zinn's home?" George asked.

"Beyond Lancaster, in the part where the Amish live."

"Tell us more about them," Bess requested.

Nancy said that Mrs. Tenney had explained that there were two types of Amish, the Church Amish, who are comparatively modern and own automobiles and electrical appliances, and the House Amish, who are very strict and do not believe in using any of these "fancy" things.

After lunch, the girls reached the outskirts of Lancaster. Nancy consulted a map. "I think this is the side road that leads to Mr. Zinn's farmhouse," she said. "Mrs. Tenney gave me rather general directions. Let's try it."

They had not gone more than a mile down the road when the car began to lurch, forcing Nancy to slow down.

"That's funny," she said, frowning. "I have plenty of gasoline, so that's not the trouble."

Suddenly the motor died and the car chugged

to a stop. The friends looked about in dismay. There was not a house in sight—nothing but open fields.

Nancy got out, raised the hood of the car, and looked for loose or broken wires. She could find none. "We're really stuck!" she announced.

"The hex is already working," Bess wailed. "Now a spell has been put on our car!"

Nancy laughed. "If so, I won't let the spell work long. We'll eliminate it, I promise you."

"I suppose the best thing to do," George said, "is to wait for a car to come along and give one of us a ride into town to find a mechanic."

Nancy agreed. "Especially if the farms nearby happen to belong to House Amish families," she said. "They won't know anything about cars."

Ten minutes went by, but no vehicle appeared. Suddenly George called out, "Here comes someone!"

The others glanced up the road. An Amish woman, wearing a black dress that reached the top of her high shoes, a black bonnet, and a white shoulder kerchief and apron, walked slowly toward them.

"Perhaps she knows somebody who can help us," Bess suggested.

To the girls' surprise, as the figure came closer, they could see that she was very young—probably no more than sixteen years old.

Nancy hastened toward the girl. "Hello," she

said. "Our car won't run. Could you tell us where we might have it fixed?"

The Amish girl was very pretty, with large brown eyes and long lashes. She smiled sweetly at Nancy.

"I am so sorry about the car," she said. "You are visitors here, ain't?"

Nancy gave her name and added that she was from River Heights. She introduced the cousins.

"I am Manda Kreutz," the girl told them. "I am walking from Lancaster."

"Lancaster?" George repeated. "That's more than ten miles from here."

Manda nodded. "It is good to walk," she said, "and I know short cuts across the fields." Then her face clouded. "I am returning to my home, but my father—maybe he will not take me back."

The girls were startled by this announcement. They also were curious to know what Manda Kreutz meant, but they did not want to embarrass her by asking for an explanation.

Apparently Manda decided to trust the three friendly visitors, as she explained, "We are Amish and my father is very strict. When I finished eighth grade, he wanted me to stay home and work on the farm. But I wanted to study more and learn about the world."

She had decided recently that perhaps this was wrong. Life was good on an Amish farm and there was never any want.

"But I did not appreciate this," she said. "I ran away from home three months ago and went to Lancaster. In the daytime I worked in a bakery and evenings I attended night school."

Wistfully she added, "But I miss my people. And yet I am so afraid my father will not let me live on the farm any more."

The three girls assured Manda that everything would probably work out, and wished her the best of luck. Nancy again asked her if she knew anyone nearby who might repair the car.

"Yes," the Amish girl replied. "Rudolph can help you. He is on a farm a mile from here."

Manda offered to stop there and ask him to bring his tool kit. Nancy thanked her, but said she would walk along with Manda and talk to Rudolph herself. Also, she was eager to learn more about the Amish people and their customs. Bess and George decided to remain with the car.

As the Amish girl and Nancy hurried along the road, Manda talked freely about her problem. "Papa is afraid if I learn too much I will not be an Amish woman any longer. But he is wrong. I might not be so strict as he is. We have no conveniences in our house or on our farm. I think that is foolish. Papa and Mama work too hard. I like learning about things, but we have no books except our German Bible and the *Gabrauch Buch*."

"What is that?" Nancy asked.

Manda explained it was something used in powwowing—a means of curing people who are ill. "Powwowing is accomplished by the 'laying on of hands.' Not everyone can make it work. But Mama can," she said proudly.

Presently a farmhouse came into sight and Manda said that this was where Rudolph lived. Her farm was beyond it.

"Why don't you wait until my car is fixed and I'll drive you home?" Nancy offered, smiling.

Manda looked frightened. "Oh, no! My Father is strict House Amish and would never forgive me if I came home in an automobile. I thank you. I will walk the rest of the way."

As the girls separated, Nancy went up the lane to Rudolph's house. A rosy-cheeked, red-haired young man wearing a straight-brimmed black hat and black homemade cloth suspenders over his red shirt saw her coming and greeted her with a bow.

"I was told by Manda Kreutz that you are an expert mechanic," Nancy said. "My car is stuck down the road. Can you help me out?"

"Ya, I will help you," he said. "I will get my car and tools." He disappeared behind the house for a few minutes, then drove out a small car. Climbing in, Nancy directed him to the stalled convertible.

When Nancy introduced the young man to

Bess and George, Rudolph said, "You are a girl? Your name is George, ain't?"

George chuckled and nodded. Rudolph remarked emphatically that among plain people, a man has a man's name and a woman, a woman's name.

The tomboyish girl did not take offense at the criticism. Laughing, she told Rudolph that she had not named herself. "But I like having a boy's name," she admitted. "It's different."

Rudolph made no further comment. He checked the car, working with amazing speed. One minute he was beneath the convertible, the next he was tinkering under the hood, and a moment later he was reaching in to the dashboard to test the ignition. Soon he announced that he had found the trouble. "The feed line —a twist in it!"

It was not long before Rudolph had fixed the car. When the girls were on their way again, Nancy decided it was too late to call on Mr. Zinn that day.

"Besides, I'd like to stop at the Kreutz farm to see how Manda made out," she went on. "If her father is as stern as she said, he may not let her stay. In that case we can take her wherever she wants to go."

The girls found the Kreutz place easily. It was a large, plain two-story house without blinds or curtains. Nearby was a large stone barn built on two levels of ground. Several other smaller buildings dotted the yard.

Nancy's knock was answered by an Amish woman who looked as if she had been crying. "You're Mrs. Kreutz?" the girl asked, smiling.

The woman nodded silently.

"Is Manda at home?" Nancy inquired.

"You know Manda?" the woman asked.

Nancy replied that she had met the Amish girl on the road and told the whole story.

Suddenly Mrs. Kreutz burst into tears. "Manda has gone again! Papa is so strict! He told Manda she could live here, but he gave orders that nobody in the family could speak to her!"

"How dreadful!" Nancy thought.

"We have six sons," Mrs. Kreutz explained. "They are married and have their own farms near here. But Papa is *mayschter*, and we obey him."

The woman looked pleadingly at Nancy. "Maybe Papa would listen to you, since you are outside our family. He will not admit to us his feelings are hurt because his only daughter has left home. Please talk to him about Manda. He is near the barn, by the bull pens."

Nancy agreed, though she had little hope she could persuade Mr. Kreutz. Bess and George joined Nancy, and the three girls walked toward the barn. They saw a large enclosure with three pens. In each stood a large black bull.

Mr. Kreutz was a giant of a man, with a ruddy complexion, sandy hair, and a long beard. He was working in the first pen.

As he heard the girls' footsteps, the farmer looked up. At the same instant the huge bull beside him lowered its horns, caught up the man, and threw him across the pen!

CHAPTER IV

Nancy's Strategy

BESS screamed. This angered the bull. With a loud snort he lowered his head as if to make a second attack on Mr. Kreutz, who lay stunned near the gate. Bess cried out again. The animal delayed his charge momentarily, eying the girl.

"Quick!" Nancy exclaimed, seeing several buckets of water standing by the barn. "Grab a pail!"

Nancy picked up one. With full force, she threw the water over the fence at the bull's head, just as he headed for the farmer again. The animal stopped dead, temporarily blinded by the water.

Then, with increased fury, he bellowed and plunged toward the motionless farmer. George now threw her water at the bull, and Nancy called to Bess, "Stand by the gate and be ready to open it when I tell you!"

Nancy grabbed another pail and heaved it into the pen. Then, reaching through the bars, she grabbed Mr. Kreutz by his shirt and dragged him forward. The bull, confused, backed up.

"Open the gate!" Nancy yelled.

As Bess obeyed, Nancy and George reached in and dragged Mr. Kreutz to safety. Bess then slammed the gate shut and locked it.

With a roar the bull rammed headfirst into the bars of his pen, trying to batter them down with his horns. Fortunately, the bars were strong.

Spying a water wheel in a sluiceway, Nancy filled another pail and hurried back to Mr. Kreutz. She dipped her handkerchief in the cold water and applied it to his forehead. Presently the man open his eyes.

"*Wuu bin ich?*" he murmured.

"You're with friends," Nancy replied, knowing he had asked where he was. "Just lie quiet for a while and you'll be all right."

Mr. Kreutz closed his eyes, but half a minute later he opened them again. Sitting up, he gazed at the three girls. Then he heard the noise of the stamping bull and this seemed to remind him of what had happened.

"How did I get here?" the farmer moaned.

"We dragged you out of the pen," George reported. "If it hadn't been for Nancy, you might have been killed by that bull."

"I remember now," Mr. Kreutz said, sitting

up. "I saw you just before the bull tossed me."

The girls helped the farmer to his feet and assisted him into the kitchen.

"Papa, Papa, what is the matter?" Mrs. Kreutz cried.

Bess explained about the bull charge.

"Ach!" the woman exclaimed.

"He'll be all right," Nancy assured her.

Mrs. Kreutz ladled out steaming soup from a huge old-fashioned kettle into a crockery bowl. While the farmer cupped the bowl in his hands and drank the hearty soup, the girls glanced about the kitchen.

One wall was taken up by a fireplace, with its traditional Dutch oven set in one side of the stonework. Above it hung copper kettles of various sizes. In the center of the fireplace was a long iron arm from which a caldron was suspended.

Beside the stove stood a box filled with logs, and the girls assumed that food was cooked over a wood fire. There was an old-fashioned sink, but no plumbing. Apparently water was carried in from the sluiceway. The bare wide-board floor had been scrubbed until it shone.

"I feel better," Mr. Kreutz announced as he set down his bowl. "Now will you girls tell me your names and why you are here?"

The girls introduced themselves. Then Mrs. Kreutz said quickly, "It's suppertime, Papa."

"We will all eat," the farmer said decisively.

The girls accepted at once and offered to help Mrs. Kreutz. Soon they sat down at a long wooden table in the kitchen, which had benches on each side. Before them were brown, yellow, and white cheeses; red, purple, and white grape jellies; a platter of huge slices of homemade bread, dishes of apple butter, stewed peaches, cherries, pickled onions, sour cantaloupe, and corn relish. For a hot dish there was boiled rabbit pot pie.

Mr. Kreutz said grace. Before eating, he asked, "Where's Manda? No place has been set for her!"

Softly his wife replied, "She has gone away again."

Mr. Kreutz stared out the window. His food went untouched and the girls sat in silence. "Eat your supper!" the man said abruptly.

The visitors began to eat, feeling ill at ease. Mrs. Kreutz did not touch her supper either. Finally she said, "Papa, you were lucky these nice girls helped you when the bull threw you."

"*Ya,* I was. *Donnk.*" He gave his curt thanks.

To ease the tension, Bess said, "It was my first meeting with a bull, and I hope the last!"

Presently the Kreutzes began to eat their supper. The guests were soon satisfied, though they had not sampled half of the various dishes.

"You have city appetites," said Mrs. Kreutz.

"All of us except Bess," George teased as her plump cousin reached for a piece of cake.

"In Amish country we like a little flesh on our maidens," Mr. Kreutz commented.

After the meal was over and they had helped with the dishes, Nancy said they must be leaving. "Do you want me to mention Manda to Mr. Kreutz?" she whispered to her hostess.

"I will fix this," the farmer's wife said. She called to her husband, "Papa, I would like for these girls to stay all night with us."

Mr. Kreutz nodded. *"Ya.* That will make our thanks for saving my life."

Mrs. Kreutz turned to Nancy and said, "Talk to him about Manda. It will be all right."

The woman did not explain further, but Nancy guessed that once an Amish person makes a promise, he keeps it. No matter what happened, the girls would spend the night there.

Nancy seated herself beside Mr. Kreutz. "Bess, George, and I met your lovely daughter on the road this afternoon," she began. "Manda was looking forward to coming home and being with her mother and father again."

The farmer shifted uneasily in his chair. "Manda is a very disobedient daughter. Amish people have rules. Our children must not break them. From the time they are small, we teach them to fear God and to work. We do not go out into the world to make money. We have security right on our own farms.

"We ask nothing from anyone," Mr. Kreutz continued proudly. "Security for an Amish man is not money. It is his family, his religion, his farm."

Nancy pondered this for a moment, then said, "You say part of your security is your family. Wouldn't you be happier if all your family were together?"

Mr. Kreutz looked directly into Nancy's eyes. "You are wise beyond your years," he said. "You have good sense."

Nancy waited eagerly for him to go on. To her surprise, Mr. Kreutz asked why she had come to Amish country.

Nancy told him about the stolen Follett furniture and explained that the thief might be somewhere around Lancaster. She also described the hex sign she had found in the mansion.

Mr. Kreutz shook his head. "Such a nice girl. I cannot understand why your papa lets you do things like this. You should be home cooking and cleaning."

At this remark, Bess and George told the Amish couple about Nancy's fine accomplishments.

"She's restored lots of people to their families," Bess explained, "and brought others peace of mind."

The farmer was silent, then he said, "If you can find missing persons, please bring my daughter home. I want her here."

Nancy promised she would do her best.

"Mind you, I do not approve of this girl-detective business," Mr. Kreutz went on, suddenly more cheerful. "Find Manda and maybe I change the mind over. Tell me what you do when you work."

"If you feel well enough to go outside, I'll be glad to give you a lesson," Nancy said, explaining that they ought to search the farm for clues to where Manda might have gone.

Mr. Kreutz said some exercise would help to ease the stiffness in his strained muscles. He took a kerosene lantern from under the closed-in sink, lighted it, and led the girls outside. Mrs. Kreutz joined them.

The Amish farmer first showed the visitors his spotless dairy. Since there was no indication that Manda had been there, the group went to the hay barn. Nancy walked back and forth with the lantern, examining every inch of the clean board floor.

"This barn is immaculate!" Bess exclaimed.

Mrs. Kreutz smiled. "We House Amish hold our religious services in the barn when there are too many people for the house," she explained. "Perhaps our barns are cleaner than our homes!"

"I'd like to climb into the loft," Nancy said. "Once when I was a little girl and got hurt on a farm we were visiting, I went to the haymow to have a good cry all by myself. Maybe Manda did the same thing."

"Go ahead," the farmer said.

Nancy scrambled up the ladder. A few moments later she called out excitedly, "I've found something!" She climbed down, holding a piece of paper. Bess and George gasped as they read: WITCH TREE.

"Do you know anything about this? Have you ever heard of a witch tree?" Nancy asked the couple.

She watched their expressions as they read the strange words and shook their heads. "It is a clue to Manda, you think?" Mr. Kreutz asked.

"Possibly," Nancy replied, "but it's like the one dropped by the furniture thief." She reminded them of the hex sign she had found at the Follett mansion.

The group inspected the rest of the buildings but found no clue to Manda's whereabouts. They returned to the house, sleepy and ready to retire.

The girls were given two upstairs rooms, which were as plair as those on the first floor. Each contained a rope double bed, two small wooden chairs, a little chest, and a curtained partition where clothes might be hung.

In the candlelight the girls saw that the furniture was gaily painted with designs of doves and flowers. The beds were covered with patchwork quilts made of pieces of vivid red, green, purple, yellow, and black cloth.

Nancy roomed alone and slept from the moment she got into bed until a crowing rooster roused her the next morning. Her mind refreshed, she began at once to think about the two puzzling mysteries. She was intrigued by the piece of paper she had found in the Kreutz hayloft. What did it mean? Manda? Hoelt? Had the two met?

When Nancy entered the cozy kitchen she asked Mr. and Mrs. Kreutz if they had ever heard of Roger Hoelt. The farmer said he had once known such a man.

"The fellow lived in Lancaster. When he was very young, I caught him in my barn stealing tools. Could this be the same man?"

Nancy said it no doubt was, because she had learned from the police that Roger Hoelt had once lived in Lancaster. She added that recently he had been imprisoned in New York as a thief.

"I suspect he's the one who stole the valuable antique furniture in our town and accidentally dropped the paper with the witch tree symbol on it. Hoelt knows I'm searching for him and has tried to scare me off the case."

Bess declared that probably it was Hoelt and not Manda who had left the witch tree symbol in the hayloft. "He's still trying to hex you, Nancy," she said, worried.

The young detective thought this was impossible as he had no way of knowing she was going to visit the Kreutzes.

The farmer looked at Bess disapprovingly. "We Amish do not believe in hexing," he said. "There are some non-Amish people in the back country who practice witchcraft."

"They do not all live in the back country, Papa," his wife spoke up. "I was talking to Mrs. Dyster at market. She told me about some people in town who think there are certain persons, especially women and girls, who practice witchcraft in secret. If these people hear that someone is a witch, they may be frightened into doing her bodily harm."

Nancy smiled. "Don't worry. My friends and I don't believe in such things," she said, looking straight at Bess.

After breakfast, the girls helped Mrs. Kreutz clean up the kitchen, then said they must be going. When they appeared in the kitchen a short time later, carrying their suitcases, Mrs. Kreutz was amazed.

"You are taking everything with you?" she asked. "Could you not stay by us while you are solving your mystery?"

"We mustn't impose," said Nancy, smiling.

Mrs. Kreutz put her hands on her hips. "Such

an idea!" she said. Then she smiled. "If you come back here each evening for supper, I can hear how you make about my daughter."

"Well, under those conditions we'll accept your invitation," said Nancy.

They would have to do some expert sleuthing, the young detective thought, to find Manda Kreutz. She had not voiced her lack of confidence, but she had a feeling that this time the Amish girl had indeed disappeared!

CHAPTER V

A Surprising Find

"WE'RE heading for Lancaster," Nancy told her friends as they drove away from the Kreutz farm. "I'd like to look for Manda, first of all."

"Let's check the bakeries there," Bess said. "I wouldn't mind a few samples!" The others laughed but agreed.

Once in Lancaster, they consulted a telephone directory and listed the town bakeries. One by one they visited them, but replies about Manda were negative until they reached Stumm Bakery.

Mrs. Stumm said that Manda had worked there until two days before. "Then she quit. Manda may have gone home or perhaps to work for those people that were in here."

"Who were they?" Nancy asked. "Can you describe them?"

"It was a couple. I think they're out-of-town Amish," the woman answered. "I gathered from their conversation that they had just moved to a farm in this area and wanted an Amish girl to help with housework."

Nancy inquired if Mrs. Stumm had ever heard Manda mention a witch tree. Looking surprised, the woman shook her head. Nancy thanked her for the information she had given, bought a bag of *fasnachts*, and left.

The young detective told her friends that she had a hunch Manda had obtained employment with this couple. Referring once more to a classified telephone book, Nancy copied names of local real-estate agents. The girls then divided the work of calling on them and met later at the car. None had found a single clue to anyone who had recently purchased a farm.

"However," Nancy said, "one man told me that old farms sometimes change hands in direct sale. We'll keep asking. Now let's go to Mr. Zinn's."

For a change George drove, and Nancy gave directions. They found Alpha Zinn's farm easily.

"We'll pretend to be interested in antiques," Nancy suggested, as the girls walked into a small building marked OFFICE.

Alpha Zinn's appearance bore out his cousin's remark about his love of eating. But the roly-poly smiling man did not look dishonest. Nancy, nevertheless, was cautious as he led the way to a large barn, where furniture was on display on the main floor and in two haylofts.

Whispering, Nancy instructed her friends to

hold the man's attention while she explored. In her purse she had a list and description of pieces taken from the Follett home. Mrs. Tenney had also provided her with a sketch of the George Washington tables.

As Nancy wandered about, she saw that Mr. Zinn's pieces were mainly pine and maple, while the articles on the list were described as dark wood. But suddenly, in a corner, she saw a small cherry table. It matched the sketch perfectly!

Meanwhile, Bess and George were asking Mr. Zinn questions about some old pewter mugs.

Abruptly, the dealer whirled around, looked for Nancy and said, "Where is your friend?"

"Maybe she's up in one of the lofts," Bess stammered.

The antique dealer eyed the cousins suspiciously. "Might she be snooping for some reason?"

At that moment Nancy hurried toward the group.

"Did you find something you like?" the chubby man asked, looking at Nancy intently.

"Yes, one piece interests me very much," the detective replied. "It's that small, unusual cherry table in the corner." She led the way back and pointed out the article.

"Oh, that," Mr. Zinn said. "It's not expensive —just a copy I made of a George Washington antique. A very good copy, I might add. I am a cabinetmaker as well as an antique dealer."

"Where is the original piece?" George asked.

"Well, actually, there are two of them," Mr. Zinn said. "One is in River Heights. I've no idea where its mate is, although I've searched and made many inquiries. I'd like to have it!"

The girls exchanged glances. Evidently Mr. Zinn did not know that Mrs. Follett had owned the matching table!

His eyes gleaming, the man went on, "The original tables have hidden drawers in them. It's said that one holds a great secret."

Nancy, Bess, and George looked startled. Did Mrs. Tenney know this? Could it be one of the reasons she suspected her cousin of taking the antique furniture?

"Please tell us more," Nancy urged.

The dealer said that the River Heights table had belonged to his recently deceased great-aunt, Mrs. Sara Follett. Her belongings were to be divided between himself and his cousin, Mrs. Tenney, a resident of that town.

He sighed. "It will be difficult to apportion the furniture, once the estate is settled. I'm sure we'll both want the Washington table. Anyway, I'm waiting to hear from the lawyer now."

"Do you think it contains the secret?" Bess asked.

"No, I purchased that antique for my aunt," Mr. Zinn said. "I learned of its secret drawer while it was in my shop being refinished. An old friend from Lancaster recognized the table from a picture he'd seen in a book of antiques. He said we ought to look for the secret compartment he'd read about, which we did. But when we finally found it, the hidden drawer was empty!"

"What a shame," George said.

"I agree. So the secret must be in the drawer of the matching antique table. That is why I'd like to find it before someone else does," the dealer concluded.

Nancy decided that it was only fair to tell Mr. Zinn what had happened. Unless he was a clever actor, he was not aware of the furniture theft. She said that she and her friends were from River Heights and his cousin was her neighbor.

"Mrs. Tenney asked me to accompany her to your great-aunt's mansion a few days ago," Nancy went on. "When we got there, we found that the place had been burglarized. The antiques in the library have been stolen!" she announced.

"What!" Mr. Zinn shouted. His face turned red and his neck muscles grew taut. "The furniture—stolen?"

"Yes," Nancy said. "But there were *two* Washington tables in the collection, according to your aunt."

"But only one was authentic," Mr. Zinn informed her. "I made the other for Aunt Sara."

The sleuth now decided to show the dealer the paper with the hex sign. He said it looked familiar, and that he had seen similar symbols.

Nancy next asked whether he knew Roger Hoelt or had ever heard of him. Mr. Zinn pondered.

"Yes, there was a fellow named Hoelt in my class in high school. But I don't think his first name was Roger," he said.

"But you do remember that people named Hoelt lived in this area?" Nancy persisted.

Mr. Zinn nodded absently, then suddenly he exclaimed, "It's a crime! All that furniture gone!"

Nancy asked whether the thief might have known of the secret drawer in the Washington table. "If so, that might have been his real motive."

"That's possible," Mr. Zinn agreed. "Particularly if he has already found the other authentic table and it didn't contain the secret. He could easily learn Aunt Sara owned its mate and in his haste, he took both of her tables with him. Maybe he couldn't distinguish the genuine from the reproduction. Oh dear, this is confusing!"

Just then a woman appeared in the barn shop. Mr. Zinn introduced her as his wife. She was as round as her husband and wore a full skirt, a shirred light-blue apron, and ruffled collar and sleeves. Her pretty face was dimpled and she had a radiant smile, which vanished when she heard the news of the robbery.

"Papa, it is a great loss to you, ain't?"

Her husband tried to hide his distress. "What

"What? Stolen!" Mr. Zinn shouted.

one does not own is never a loss," he told her, "and perhaps the furniture will be found."

"Papa, I came to tell you that dinner is ready," Mrs. Zinn said. She added, "It would please us to have you girls break bread with us."

"Oh, that would be wonderful!" Bess exclaimed. Nancy and George also accepted.

Mrs. Zinn led the way into the farmhouse. It was gayer than that of the Kreutzes, with flowers, window draperies, and quaint hooked rugs in every room. The cloth on the kitchen table was hand-embroidered with red and blue pigeons.

Mrs. Zinn set three more places at the table, and soon the five were eating a hearty meal. The dessert was shoofly pie. Between courses, the Zinns asked where the girls were staying.

When they told them, Mrs. Zinn frowned. "Mr. Kreutz is too strict," she complained. "He never allowed Manda to have a good time. He said he would pick her a husband. That's why she ran away. You know she ran away?"

Nancy nodded and said that Mr. Kreutz now wanted his daughter to come home, and that the girls had promised to help find her. She told of the clue the bakery woman had suggested, but the Zinns did not know of any new Amish couple in town.

An hour later Nancy and her friends were on their way back to the Kreutz farm. Bess, looking out the rear window, suddenly declared that she thought they were being followed by a car.

"Maybe the hex is working again," she said.

George, disgusted, told her cousin to stop talking nonsense. Suddenly a horn blasted. Nancy pulled into a service station and the car shot past them so quickly that the girls caught only a glimpse of the Amish driver. He was bearded and his black hat was pulled far down over his ears.

"That speed demon didn't follow us long," George observed.

When Nancy's car was refueled, they set out again. As she rounded a sharp turn, she suddenly gasped and stepped on the brake. Strewn across the road, directly in their path, were cinder blocks. There was no way to avoid plowing into them!

The car hit several of the blocks. All three girls were thrown forward. Bess, seated in the middle, struck her head on the mirror and blacked out!

CHAPTER VI

Witches

QUICKLY Nancy stopped the car. She and George got out and laid the unconscious girl on the front seat of the convertible.

As they leaned over Bess, worried, their friend raised her eyelids and blinked. Then she gingerly tried to sit up.

"Ow!" she moaned, sinking down again and putting a hand to her forehead. "I certainly gave my head a bang!"

"All of us might have been killed!" George cried indignantly. "Who could have been so careless?"

Nancy noticed an excavation for a building and a neat pile of the cinder blocks off to the side. She declared that the obstruction seemed to have been caused by more than carelessness. "I think it was done deliberately!"

"The hex is at fault," Bess muttered, sitting up cautiously.

Nancy and George carried the blocks out of the way so they could drive on. Bess sat and watched them through the open door of the car. Suddenly a piece of paper stuck between two of the blocks caught her eye.

Bess got out and picked up the paper. There was writing on it.

"Listen!" she cried, and read, " 'Nancy Drew, witches are not wanted in Amish country.' "

Nancy and George rushed to Bess's side and read the note themselves.

"This explains a lot," Nancy said. "I bet that man who passed us was Roger Hoelt in disguise! He knew these blocks were here and threw them into the road and left this note!"

The cousins gasped. "You're right," said George, "and we're after him. Come on!"

The girls quickly got into the car and started off. Bess remarked that the man had such a head start they would never be able to find him.

"We'll watch for his tire tracks in the dust," Nancy said. She thought it should be easy to trail the man, for the road was not well traveled and was extremely dusty.

As they rode along, Nancy said she had a new slant on the case. The couple for whom Manda might be working were Roger Hoelt and his wife.

"You mean they're posing as an Amish couple?" George asked.

"Yes. Since he once lived here, he'd know just how to do it."

"I agree. But how long are we going to follow these tracks?" Bess asked.

"If we don't catch him by the time we get to the highway, we're out of luck," Nancy replied. "This road leads into it, according to the map, and Hoelt's trail will disappear once he's on the pavement."

The girls sped along for nearly a mile in that direction, but did not overtake the suspect.

Finally Bess pleaded that they give up the chase. "I have a dreadful headache," she said.

"Why didn't you tell me before?" Nancy asked kindly. "We'll go right back to Kreutzes'."

At the farm, Manda's mother greeted the girls eagerly. "Did you find any trace of my daughter?"

Nancy alighted from the car and told the woman about the Amish couple for whom Manda might be working. "Tomorrow we'll try to locate them," she promised.

Mrs. Kreutz looked at Bess, who was being helped out of the car. "Why, look at your head!" she cried solicitously. "What happened?"

"We had to stop suddenly and I bumped it," Bess replied.

Nancy told Mrs. Kreutz about the cinder blocks

that had been thrown in the road, and said she had been unable to avoid hitting them. But she did not mention the note or her suspicions regarding the Hoelts.

They all went into the house and George asked, "Have you something we can put on Bess's head? It's aching badly."

"Yes, I have some homemade liniment," Mrs. Kreutz replied. "But I will do a little powwowing too. Come upstairs."

Bringing the bottle of liniment and a cloth to Bess's bedroom, she told the girl to lie down. She sprinkled the folded cloth with the liniment and placed it on Bess's forehead. Then she went for her *Gabrauch Buch*.

In a low voice, Mrs. Kreutz began to read from the book in German. She gently stroked Bess's head, then her arms. Finally the woman closed her eyes and began to mumble to herself. Nancy and George wondered if she were praying. A few minutes later Bess sighed, closed her eyes, and went to sleep.

Mrs. Kreutz seemed to be unaware of anything but her powwow. But presently she stopped speaking, rose, and motioned to Nancy and George to follow her from the bedroom.

"Bess will feel better now," the woman said.

Downstairs, Mrs. Kreutz's mood changed abruptly. Smiling, she asked the two girls if they would like to help her prepare supper. "We will have moon pies tonight," she said.

"And I'll bet they'll taste out of this world," George said with a laugh.

"That is a good joke," Mrs. Kreutz said. "And I suppose you never heard of them. Come. We will prepare a dozen."

The woman rolled the piecrust dough out on a table and floured it. Then she told the girls to cut it into round sections six inches in diameter. This done, she asked George to go outside to the small stone house through which a stream of cold water flowed. Here crocks of milk, cream, cheeses, and meats were kept cool.

"Bring the roast of veal," the woman directed. "It stands behind on the top shelf over."

When George returned with the meat, Mrs. Kreutz cut a generous piece from it. She put this into a wooden chopping bowl and cut it up fine with an old-fashioned chopper.

The meat was now transferred to a skillet on the stove. Butter, cream, salt, pepper, and pickled relish were added. After it had cooked a while, Mrs. Kreutz directed the girls to butter the rounds of dough. Into half of each she put generous spoonfuls of the meat mixture.

"Now pull the lids over and pinch the edges all around with your thumbs," she instructed.

"They look like half-moons!" George declared.

Mrs. Kreutz spread more butter on top of

each, and said the moon pies were ready for the oven. "Papa likes these for supper," she said. "By the way, do not mention Manda to Papa. When he is ready to talk about her, he will ask you."

Within an hour, Bess came downstairs, saying she felt much better. "And doesn't something smell good! Mm-mm!"

George laughed. "Bess must be back to normal. She's hungry!" She told her cousin of Mrs. Kreutz's request not to mention Manda.

During the meal Mr. Kreutz did not bring up the subject of his missing daughter. But as soon as the dishes had been washed, he called Nancy aside and asked her what she had learned about Manda.

Nancy told him in detail, and added, "Mr. Kreutz, I think you should notify the police. They may be able to locate Manda easily."

"No!" Mr. Kreutz cried loudly. "I am an Amish man. We take care of family matters without the help of the police. I gave you my permission to locate my daughter. But no one outside the family, except you three, will be allowed to interfere."

The farmer then asked Nancy what else she and her friends had done that day. When the girl described the accident and the note in the cinder block, Mr. Kreutz exclaimed, *"Du bin en hex maydel!"*

"I'm not a witch!" Nancy protested, amazed

that evidently he now believed the superstition.

Despite her denial, Mr. and Mrs. Kreutz at once became cool toward all the girls. The farmer said it was time to go to bed, and they both nodded a curt good night and left the room.

The girls, nonplussed by the change in their hosts' attitude, spoke in whispers. "This settles it," said Bess. "We'll move out in the morning."

"Yes, we're certainly not wanted," George agreed. "Imagine their believing that you're a witch, Nancy!"

Their friend, with a mystified expression, asked herself, "But why are the Kreutzes so convinced all of a sudden that I am a witch? There's something to this they haven't told us!"

CHAPTER VII

A Stolen Horse

THE sudden change in the attitude of the Kreutzes toward the girls bothered them so much that they slept fitfully. The farmer had said he did not believe in hexing, yet when Nancy had shown him the note about witches, he had acted as if she were one!

"If people around this area are going to be afraid of me," Nancy thought, "I'll have a difficult time trying to solve the mystery."

Although Nancy did not intend to give up the case because of such an attitude, Bess was of a different frame of mind. Sensitive by nature, she did not want to stay where she would be shunned. Besides, she felt that further work on the mystery would involve more danger all the time.

"I'll try to talk Nancy into leaving this Amish country," she decided.

As for George, she was angry with the Kreutzes.

After Nancy and her friends had made their best efforts to locate a girl who had run away, her parents were now treating their guests as suspects!

Early the following morning, Nancy and the girls packed their bags and went downstairs. Mr. and Mrs. Kreutz were already at the table, having breakfast. They nodded, but did not invite the girls to join them.

"We're leaving," said Nancy. "I'm sorry that you've been disturbed by rumors about me and that you evidently believe them. I strongly suspect that Roger Hoelt is behind all of this. Some day he'll be caught, then I'll be cleared of these silly charges."

Nancy's hope that her words might convince Mr. and Mrs. Kreutz was not fulfilled. The farmer and his wife merely nodded again, and did not rise or even say good-by. Nevertheless, each of the girls thanked the couple for their hospitality, then walked out the kitchen door. In silence they got into Nancy's convertible and drove off.

"Well, I've never been so badly treated by nice people in all my life!" George stormed.

"Maybe we shouldn't blame them too much," Nancy suggested. "There may be more to this than we realize. But I intend to find out what it is!"

"Will you keep on looking for Manda?" Bess asked Nancy.

"Certainly. If she's working for a thief, I want to warn her as soon as possible."

"Maybe," Bess surmised, "the Kreutzes think you know where Manda is and won't tell them."

"That's possible. They may have been told a witch is responsible for Manda's disappearance and now they believe I'm that person."

"I'd like to bet," said George, "that if we bring Manda back, the Kreutzes will do an about-face."

Bess wanted to know where Nancy was heading. Nancy said she thought they might try New Holland. It was a good base from which to work.

"I'd like to make some inquiries around that area."

In New Holland they found a place to eat and ordered breakfast.

"We'd better keep this witch business to ourselves," Nancy advised, "or we may not find a place to sleep."

Bess and George smiled, and Nancy asked the woman in charge if she could recommend a boardinghouse. The woman suggested a place about a mile out of town.

"Papa Glick had a bad accident two years ago and had to give up farming," the woman said. "Now he is a *schumacher*. Mama Glick will rent rooms sometimes. The Glicks are Church Amish. You will be very comfortable there."

When the visitors finished eating, they went directly to the farm. It was well kept, although many of the fields were in pasture. The house was of red brick. The wooden barn was also red.

A pleasant-faced woman, wearing a green dress and the traditional Amish cap and apron, opened the door. When Nancy stated the reason for the girls' call, Mrs. Glick invited them in.

"I have four rooms empty," she said. "Make your choice between."

The interior of the house, with its homespun draperies and floor coverings, was quaint and attractive. The second-floor bedrooms were spanking clean and just as cheerful. The girls were delighted and at once chose the rooms they would take.

"You are sightseeing in New Holland?" Mrs. Glick asked.

"Yes, we are," Nancy replied. Feeling she could confide in this pleasant woman, she added, "And we're also here for another reason." She told Mrs. Glick about the stolen furniture for which they were looking and their suspicion that the thief might be hiding in Amish territory.

At this moment the girls heard footsteps on the stairs and a boy and girl appeared. Mrs. Glick introduced them as Becky, aged ten, her daughter, and Henner, eight, her son.

"They're adorable, and how healthy looking!" Bess exclaimed.

Both children had big brown eyes and very straight bodies. Their hair was cut and combed in the Amish style.

Becky wore a prayer cap just like her mother's and carried a black bonnet over her arm. She wore a long black smock with a white blouse underneath, and a white apron but no kerchief.

Henner held an Amish boy's hat in his hand. The boy's blue shirt, black trousers, and wide homemade suspenders were exactly the same as those the girls had seen all the Amish men wearing.

"Henner," said his mother, "I'm sorry to see you so dirty when we have visitors. Did you fall?"

His sister answered for him. "Henner, he goes by horse stall down. *Iss er net schuslich?*"

"Yes, he is careless," his mother agreed. "Henner, go scrub yourself."

The girls went downstairs to get their luggage and then unpacked. Half an hour later they were ready to take up their sleuthing.

Just as Nancy, Bess, and George were leaving, they heard hoofbeats and saw an Amish carriage coming up the lane. The horse's sleek body gleamed and so did the highly varnished black vehicle he was pulling. The carriage was plain, with no dashboard or other trimming. It had a front and rear seat, and was almost completely enclosed.

"Papa kumpt hame!" the children cried, and ran to meet him.

Mrs. Glick went outside with the girls and introduced her husband, a nice-looking kindly man, but pale compared to Amish farmers they had seen.

After greeting him, Nancy told Mr. Glick what had brought the girls to Pennsylvania Dutch country. The cobbler had not heard of Roger Hoelt, and was sorry to learn about the stolen furniture.

"Mr. and Mrs. Glick, do you know Manda Kreutz?" Nancy asked.

The couple exchanged glances, then Papa Glick said, "Yes," and added, "We do not approve of young girls running away from home. But maybe her father was too strict. Now she has taken up with Amish strangers."

"Please tell me about it," Nancy begged. "Where is Manda?"

"I do not know," Mr. Glick replied. "But she was seen riding in a carriage with a couple who told a friend of mine, Mr. Weiss, they are from Ohio."

"Is he sure they are Amish?" Nancy inquired.

"My friend wonders," the cobbler answered, "because of their speech. He thinks they might be English."

When Nancy inquired what Mr. Glick meant by the last remark, he explained that among his sect, any non-Amish people were called English, meaning foreigners.

"This pair wore Amish clothing," he said, "and

had an Amish carriage, but maybe they were just putting on."

Nancy was excited over this latest piece of information. Her hunch had probably been right. The couple were Mr. and Mrs. Roger Hoelt! If Manda Kreutz became too friendly with them, she might get into serious trouble with the law!

"We're trying to find Manda," Nancy told the Glicks. "I know it's hard to believe but her father has had a change of heart and now both parents want their daughter to come home. Can you give us any other clues?" she asked the cobbler. He regretfully said no.

Nancy had a sudden inspiration. "If the Hoelts are masquerading," she said aloud, "they probably bought a horse and carriage around here recently."

"Unless they stole them," George interposed.

"That could easily be done," Mrs. Glick spoke up. "Amish carriages all look alike. It is difficult to distinguish one from another."

Then she smiled a little. "The owners have funny ways of telling them apart—a bullet hole from rifle practice or a high board on the floor for a short-legged wife."

Mr. Glick insisted that an owner did not even need earmarks to tell his carriage from others. "We *chust* look at 'em. We know 'em!" he said. "Nobody can fool us."

Nancy told Mr. Glick that she suspected the man masquerading as Amish might be the furniture thief, and she would like to inquire at local carriage factories about any recent purchase by an out-of-state man. The cobbler gave her the name of a factory five miles away, and the girls set off at once for the place. There Nancy spoke to the manager and stated the reason for her call.

"You have come to the right place," the man said. "But the carriage was not purchased. It was stolen!"

"Stolen!" Nancy gasped.

"Do you know who took it?" the manager asked.

"No. By the way, have you ever met Roger Hoelt?"

"Never heard of him."

Nancy remarked that maybe the thief had also stolen a horse to go with the carriage.

"You have the nail on the head hit," the man said. "My uncle, who lives a few miles from here, has a lot of horses. He missed one the same day my carriage was stolen."

"Quite a coincidence," Nancy declared. "What color was the horse?"

"Black."

"Thank you very much, sir. You've been very helpful."

Nancy excitedly hurried outside to tell Bess

and George what she had learned. They, too, were enthusiastic about the latest development.

"So now," said George, "we start roaming the countryside, looking for a fake Amish man driving a black horse and carriage." She chuckled. "Who wants the honor of pulling off his false beard?"

CHAPTER VIII

Disturbing Rumors

"There's one thing I'm glad of," Bess said as the girls drove back toward New Holland. "We don't have to return to the Kreutzes' and tell them that their daughter has taken up with a thief."

"If Manda really is with the Hoelts," Nancy stated, "I'm sure she has no idea that they're thieves."

George pointed out that the Amish girl might have to testify in court if the Hoelts were apprehended. "That would crush her proud parents," she said.

Presently Nancy noticed that they were near the road that led to the Zinn house. She suggested they stop and tell Mr. Zinn what they had learned about the Hoelts. He might have additional news for them.

"He has no idea where we're staying now in

case he should want to get in touch with us," Nancy reminded them.

The girls found the antique dealer wearing a broad smile. "I've sold many pieces of furniture since yesterday morning," Mr Zinn said. "And at good prices. Well, have you any news of the stolen antiques?"

Before Nancy could reply, he went on, "You remember that cherry table you were interested in—the George Washington copy?"

As the girls nodded, Mr. Zinn continued, "It was one of the articles I sold." He chuckled. "A couple came in and asked about it. I named a high price, expecting them to bargain with me. But they bought the table then and there.

"Funny about that couple," he continued. "Amish, but they don't live around here. Came from Ohio. A long distance to drive in a carriage."

Nancy, Bess, and George were astonished.

"Was it drawn by a black horse?" Nancy asked.

"Yes," said Mr. Zinn. "Why?"

Nancy told him of her suspicions that Hoelt was masquerading. "It's likely he found out the George Washington tables he stole don't contain the secret," Nancy deduced.

Mr. Zinn chuckled. "And because of the high price I set on my copy of the table, he figured it must be the genuine matching piece."

"Exactly."

"You mean I had the thief who stole my inheritance right in my shop and I let him get away?" The antique dealer's face grew red with anger.

"I'm afraid so," Nancy said. She had a sudden hunch. "How did this man pay for the table?"

"In cash. Big bills," Mr. Zinn replied.

"May I see them?" the girl requested.

The man unlocked his old-fashioned roll-top desk and took out a tin box. From this he removed five 20-dollar bills.

Nancy took a similar bill from her pocket and held it next to Mr. Zinn's money. First, she compared the letter, plate, and serial numbers, and the series identification. All seemed to be in order. Next, she compared the paper quality, since she knew that genuine United States currency has a distinctive feel. They were identical as far as she could tell.

While the group watched breathlessly, Nancy examined the scrollwork on the border of the front and back plates of each note. Now she frowned—in this respect they were lacking in continuity and uniformity of shading.

"Look!" she exclaimed, pointing out the difference between the five 20-dollar bills, and the sharp clarity of her own.

Mr. Zinn cried out, "Those bills the man gave me—is counterfeit *gelt?*"

"Yes, I'm pretty sure they are." Nancy sighed.

The man paced back and forth in his office. Finally Nancy asked him if he were going to call the police to report the counterfeit money.

"*Ya, ya,*" the dealer said. He fumbled through the telephone book and then handed it to Nancy, asking her to find the number of the police station.

Nancy made the call. The local police captain said he would send an expert down at once to examine the money.

In a short time two officers arrived. One immediately said the bills were fake. The other policeman wrote down a description of the couple who had bought the table.

"We'll send a report to the state troopers," one of the officers said. "We ought to pick up the two of them in no time."

The girls stayed to wait for a report. But hours passed and there was no news from the police. Late in the afternoon they were looking at several patchwork quilts Mrs. Zinn had made with the help of her neighbors, when her husband rushed into the house.

"Where's Nancy Drew?" he shouted.

Mrs. Zinn and the visitors hurried to the kitchen, where the antique dealer stood with his feet apart and his hands on his hips. "So this is how you work!" he cried. "You come around here pretending to be friends, and this is what you're up to!"

Nancy hardly knew what to reply but finally she asked him what he meant.

"As if you didn't know," he said, shaking a finger at her. "But you've been found out! You thought you could get away with those two valuable lamps of mine, but you didn't do it!"

The young detective stared. Had the man gone out of his mind? George, now angered, demanded that the dealer explain his accusations.

"Those two lamps in your car!" Mr. Zinn roared. "How long have they been there? The woman told me you're a witch and now I believe it!"

It was several minutes before Mrs. Zinn could calm her husband enough for him to give an explanation. A woman had telephoned to warn him that a girl by the name of Nancy Drew, who looked very innocent, was really a witch and a thief. She was riding about the countryside stealing small valuable antiques.

"The woman told me," said Zinn, "that if I looked in your car I would no doubt find something from my shop. Well, I did. Nancy Drew, I'm going to call the police!"

Nancy did not raise her voice, although she too was becoming angry. "Did the woman who called give her name?"

The antique dealer glared. "No, she didn't. But she was right. I found my stolen lamps hidden under a blanket on the back seat of your car. How can you explain that?"

"I'm sure this is Roger Hoelt's work," Nancy declared. "He planted the lamps there and got his wife to make the call. It's one of the ways he's been trying to keep me from working on the case."

Bess was indignant at the man's continued anger. "Nancy is not only trying to find the thief who robbed your aunt's estate but has also taught you something about accepting money too hastily from strangers!" she said hotly.

Finally, Mr. Zinn became calmer and said he would not call the police. But he said firmly that he wanted the girls to leave immediately.

"That suits me," said George. "If we had wanted to take your old lamps, don't you think we'd have left long before this?"

The girls walked to the convertible and drove off without a backward glance.

All three were deeply disturbed. Roger Hoelt had played a clever trick in accusing Nancy of being a thief. She was becoming more unpopular by the moment in the Amish community. Soon no one would be willing to trust the young detective.

Bess was afraid that if Mr. Zinn spread the story of the lamps, the girls might even be asked to leave the county. "By the time we return to the Glicks', they may freeze up too, and turn us out," she prophesied dolefully.

It was with some apprehension that the girls drove up to the Glick farmhouse. Becky and Henner rushed out to meet them. Henner called out, "You be witches, ain't?"

Nancy got out of the car and put her arms around the little boy. Quietly but firmly, she told him that she and her friends were not witches. "Pinch me and see," she suggested.

"But Mama, she went to a *schnitzing*," Henner told her. "The women say you all be witches."

At this moment Mrs. Glick ran from the house. Having overheard her son's remark, she scolded him. "I told you that witches are only make-believe. You are a bad boy for repeating what I told your papa those silly women said. Go help him now!"

Mrs. Glick turned to the girls as her children ran off. "Some of my friends are superstitious," she said. "They forget that witches are nothing but old wives' tales!"

They all went into the house and Nancy excused herself to freshen up for supper. Alone, she reviewed her problem. Roger Hoelt and his wife were undoubtedly the source of the vicious rumors. But how to cope with them was the big question.

Just then she heard a car coming up the lane.

Peering from the window, Nancy saw a state trooper.

A few moments later Mrs. Glick called to her, "Nancy, will you come downstairs, please?"

Nancy fairly flew to the first floor, hoping that the trooper had some news of Roger Hoelt and his wife. Mrs. Glick introduced her to the officer, a freckle-faced outdoor-type man.

"How do you do?" the officer acknowledged the introduction. "Well, you certainly don't look much like a witch!"

Nancy was thunderstruck. Was he joking, or did the police believe the foolish rumors, too?

The trooper grinned and explained that earlier in the day a call had been received at police headquarters. An unidentified woman had said that three out-of-state girls were trouble-makers —and witches! She said one in particular, Nancy Drew, had claimed she had supernatural powers, enabling her to locate missing persons and solve mysteries.

The trooper smiled. "We know it's nonsense. But our practice is to investigate anonymous calls whenever possible. I traced you here. Can you clear this up, Miss Drew?"

Nancy told the officer everything that had happened, and for the first time Mrs. Glick heard the story of the hex sign. Nancy admitted she had solved several mysteries, but said that she did not claim to be an expert. She added that she had not tried to cause trouble.

The officer was satisfied and departed, wishing the young detective good luck.

Mrs. Glick came to Nancy's side and laid a motherly hand on her shoulder. "Tomorrow you are going to forget the mystery and have a good time. It is market day. Would you girls like to help me stand market?"

"Oh, we'd love to!" Nancy cried, her face brightening. "What can we do for you?"

The farm woman said that the vegetables had to be picked after sundown, washed, and arranged attractively. "Early tomorrow we will bake bread and make pies and cakes to sell."

The family and their visitors had an early supper. Then Mrs. Glick and all the girls went into the garden and began picking plump carrots and beets. When their baskets were full, they carried them to the sluiceway and washed the vegetables, which were then sorted according to size, cleaned, and tied into bunches.

At last the girls, tired from the long day, tumbled into bed. It seemed they had hardly fallen asleep when Mrs. Glick knocked on their doors. "It is four o'clock. Time to get up!"

The three jumped out of bed, hurried into their clothes, and raced downstairs. They found Mrs. Glick busy with her baking. From the oven came the aroma of apple pie and cookies.

"You are sleepy birds," Mrs. Glick teased, while stirring batter for a cake. "But you are in time to make the *fasnachts.*"

When the hot fat was ready, Nancy and George dropped the raw doughnut rings into it, one by one. As soon as each was cooked, it was removed and dried on paper. Bess sprinkled them with powdered sugar.

"When you get hungry, help yourselves," Mrs. Glick invited. "We will not have time to sit down to breakfast."

"We'll leave at six sharp," Mrs. Glick announced, as she bustled about the homey kitchen. After a snack, the girls assisted her in packing the food into her automobile.

When they reached the market, the visitors helped Mrs. Glick set up her stall. Afterward, the woman suggested that they walk through the market and look around the town.

The three friends were intrigued, not only by the hearty, appetizing foods and the bright flowers on display but also by the hand needlework and cookbooks on sale.

Outside the market, Nancy, Bess, and George watched Amish carriage after carriage arrive. There was a long row of hitching posts to which the horses were tied side-by-side. There was not a black horse among them. Most of the men and women were tall and strong looking. All had good color and bright eyes.

George suddenly grinned. "The minute they turn their backs, you can't tell one from another."

Bess giggled. "The young men must have a hard time keeping track of their dates!"

An hour later the girls decided to return to the market. As they turned the corner they saw an Amish girl coming toward them.

Suddenly Nancy cried out, "Why it's Manda Kreutz!"

CHAPTER IX

Mistaken Identity

NANCY and her chums stopped in front of Manda Kreutz on the street, but the Amish girl looked at them blankly. She gave no sign of recognition.

Ignoring this, Bess said to her sweetly, "Why did you run away from home again?"

"I think you must have me mixed up with someone else," the girl replied. She started to walk on.

Nancy took her arm. "Surely you remember us—the girls who met you on the road when you were walking home from Lancaster?"

Suddenly the Amish girl smiled. "I guess you have mistaken me for my cousin, Manda Kreutz."

The three friends were stunned. Now that they looked closely at the stranger before them, they knew she was not Manda. This young woman was slightly shorter and plumper. But otherwise the cousins looked enough alike to be identical twins.

"Well, I surely thought you were Manda," Nancy said, smiling. She introduced herself, Bess, and George. "We met your cousin the other day and have been trying to find her ever since."

"I'll tell you where she lives," the Amish girl said. "By the way, my name is Melinda Kreutz."

George spoke. "We know where Manda's family lives, but she is not living at home. Didn't you know this, Melinda?"

"No," the Amish girl replied. Then, looking at the others searchingly, she said, "Is something the matter?"

Bess answered quickly. "You mean you don't know Manda has run away from home?"

"*Sell iss awschrecklich!*" Then Melinda added quickly, "I beg your pardon. You do not understand our language. I mean, it is dreadful. I did not know about Manda, for I do not hear from my cousin often. Our ways are different. I am Church Amish."

After hearing the story, she shook her head. "My uncle is too stern but he loves his family. Soon, though, Manda would have married and gone away from home, anyhow. She should not have run away."

"You mean Manda has wedding plans?" Bess asked.

"No. There was no young man I've heard of. But all Amish girls marry young," Melinda explained.

Melinda was glad that Manda's father had decided to forgive her and take her back. She hoped that Nancy and her friends would soon find her cousin.

"Can you give us any hint as to where she may be?" the young detective asked. "We heard she was working for an Amish couple who have recently moved into this area."

Melinda studied the sidewalk for several moments. Then she looked up and said, "This may help you. Two days ago a man hurried up to me on the street and began to talk. I guess he thought I was Manda."

Nancy asked what he looked like. The girl's description fitted Roger Hoelt in Amish disguise.

"Did he say anything to give you an idea of where Manda might be?" George prodded.

Melinda said that the man had rushed up to her and cried out in Pennsylvania Dutch, "You've got to get out of here quick and go back to the *schnitz!* That witch girl is coming!"

Nancy was furious. Roger Hoelt had convinced Manda that Nancy was a witch!

"Please go on, Melinda," she requested as calmly as she could.

Melinda said she had told the man that she

did not know what he was talking about. He had tried to argue with her and had said, "You can't run out on my wife and me like that!"

But when Melinda had insisted that she did not know him, a frightened look suddenly came over his face. He had mumbled something about thinking she was someone else and had gone off.

"What do you think the man meant by his strange words?" Melinda asked Nancy.

The detective smiled. "I don't know, Melinda. You should know better than I. What is a *schnitz?*"

Melinda said it was a word with variations of meaning, but that it had to do with apples. In recipes such as *schnitz un gnepp,* it meant dried apples and dumplings. A *schnitzing* was an apple paring and drying party.

"Well, how would you interpret what the man said to you about going back to the *schnitz?*" George asked Melinda.

The Amish girl thought it might mean a *schnitzing.* "I would like to know who the witch girl is."

"I can't tell you," Nancy replied quickly. Then the three girls said good-by and hurried off.

"Well, we picked up a good clue, even though we didn't find Manda," Bess remarked.

"A very good clue," Nancy agreed. "Now we must locate someone who knows where the *schnitz* is." She asked a policeman, but he could not help her.

The visitors returned to the market and walked among the stalls until they came to Mrs. Glick's stand. To their amazement, she had sold nearly everything she had brought from the farm.

"A couple more pie sales and I shall be able to return home," she said, smiling.

"That's fine," Nancy said. Then she told Mrs. Glick how they had mistaken Melinda Kreutz for Manda. "Do you know where the *schnitz* is?" she asked.

Mrs. Glick had never heard of it. "We ask Papa when we get home," she said. "I'll be ready to leave in about half an hour."

Nancy turned to her friends and suggested they walk around town again and keep an eye open for Roger Hoelt. "Evidently he does come into town. I presume he relies on his disguise to avoid being identified."

The girls were about ready to rejoin Mrs. Glick when Bess suddenly spied a black horse and carriage in front of a bakery.

"Look!" she cried. At the same moment a slender middle-aged Amish woman came from the shop and got into the carriage.

"Do you suppose that could be Mrs. Hoelt?" Bess asked eagerly.

"There's one way to find out," Nancy replied,

and she dashed into the bakery to ask the woman's identity.

"That was Mrs. Esch," the girl behind the counter told Nancy.

"Has she lived here a long time?" Nancy inquired.

"Oh, yes," the clerk said.

Returning to her friends, Nancy sighed and said, "Another false lead."

As the three girls walked back to the market, Bess again cried out, "Look down the road! There's another black horse and Amish carriage."

Nancy, Bess, and George rushed toward it. But just as they were almost near enough to see the driver, he started up. The man looked fleetingly in their direction, then slapped his horse, and it galloped off down the road.

"That was the same man who passed us the other day!" George cried. "He's Roger Hoelt! Come on! We must catch him!"

Nancy's first thought was to run to Mrs. Glick's car and give chase. But she did not have the ignition key. By the time she could get it, Hoelt would be out of sight.

"I'll report this to the policeman over there," she said, and hurried up to him. Nancy gave the officer the details of the mystery quickly.

"I have orders not to leave my beat," the officer said reluctantly. "I'm sorry, miss. Why don't you go to police headquarters and report your suspicion to them?"

He gave her directions, and the three girls hurried off. Suddenly Nancy stopped. Headquarters was five blocks away and by the time they reached it Roger Hoelt would have pulled off the road and hidden somewhere.

"Let's not report anything," she suggested. "Next time we see Hoelt we'll have more to go on. I hate making a nuisance of ourselves to the police."

Nancy, Bess, and George returned to Mrs. Glick, who was sorry to learn they had missed catching the thief. The group drove home, and Nancy at once asked Mr. Glick if he had ever heard of the *schnitz*.

The cobbler scratched his head and thought for nearly a minute. Then finally he said, "At one time there was a farm somewhere around here that had an apple-drying business. Maybe it was called the *schnitz*, although I never heard any name for it."

Mr. Glick did not know its exact location but would inquire of his neighbors. Nancy drove with him to several farms in the area. No one they asked had ever heard of the *schnitz*.

At each place Nancy also showed the drawing of the witch tree symbol. Since none of these people had ever seen it, she came to the conclusion it was a hex sign used only by Hoelt. He had probably designed it himself.

"Well," she told herself philosophically, "if I ever do come across it on a barn or house I'll expect to find Hoelt there!"

During the evening Mr. and Mrs. Glick entertained the girls with stories of their younger days.

The three girls slept well and were up early the next morning to continue their sleuthing. It was a beautiful day and they walked outside with Mr. Glick for some fresh air before breakfast.

Suddenly the farmer cried out, *Ach, ya! Waas gayt aw?"*

At the same instant, the girls saw what he was looking at—the witch tree symbol had been painted on the side of the barn!

Underneath it was a picture of a witch riding a broom. No wonder the farmer had said, "What goes here?" The face of the witch bore a strong resemblance to that of Nancy Drew!

CHAPTER X

A Disastrous Race

COMPLETELY dumfounded, Nancy, Bess, and George continued to stare at the crudely made markings on the Glick barn. They were sure that Roger Hoelt or some friend of his had painted the witch symbol on the building, probably by flashlight during the night.

The startling likeness of the witch's face to Nancy's made Bess fearful. "We just can't stay here!" she murmured. "Nancy, please give up this case. That awful man is going to harm you!"

"Shh," Nancy warned her. "Look at Becky and Henner!"

The two children were standing in the doorway of the farmhouse, whispering to each other. They scooted back into the kitchen.

Immediately Mrs. Glick appeared outside. Seeing the marks on the barn, she hurried toward

her husband and the girls. None of them had
made a comment since Bess's outburst, but now
Mr. Glick said firmly, "Your enemy is a very bad
and dangerous man, Nancy. He must be made to
stop frightening people. There is no room in
Amish country for such a person."

Nancy heartily agreed and said that instead of
leaving she would double her efforts to locate
Roger Hoelt.

"That is good," the cobbler said. "But take
care."

Mrs. Glick called her children outside and
scolded them for being afraid. "How many times
have I told you there are no witches?" she said
sternly. "Come now. Shake hands with Nancy
Drew and say you are sorry for running away
from her."

Becky and Henner moved forward obediently,
but their approach was timid. Nancy held out her
arms to them, suggesting that they help her paint
out the silly figures on the barn. Pleased by the
suggestion, the two children laughed and ran
toward Nancy.

"Can we work right now?" Henner asked. "I
want to paint away the witch."

Mr. Glick nodded, saying the sooner the figures
were removed, the better. "No breakfast for the
three of you until the picture is all over painted,"
he said.

Henner went to the barn and returned with a can of red paint and three brushes. Mrs. Glick provided a ladder for Nancy to use. The girl detective and the children started to work.

Bess and George returned to the house to help Mrs. Glick prepare breakfast. Soon Nancy and the children had finished painting, and everyone sat down to eat.

A few minutes later the telephone rang. Mrs. Glick answered it and called Nancy. "It's your father," she announced.

Nancy had sent her father the Glicks' address. She hurried to the phone, worried that something was wrong.

"Hello, Nancy dear, I have to go out of town for a couple of days and I wanted to let you know," her father said. "Hannah will visit her sister, unless you are coming right home."

"Dad, I'm sorry to tell you that I'm not getting along very fast on this mystery," Nancy advised. "I won't be home for several days." She brought her father up to date.

"If you change your plans, let Hannah know," the lawyer directed. "By the way, you're all going to have company this afternoon."

"Here?"

"Yes."

"How nice," Nancy said. "Who?"

Mr. Drew replied that it was to be a surprise.

He wished his daughter good luck and said good-by.

When Nancy returned to the table and told Bess and George they could all expect company, they began to guess who it might be.

"Mrs. Tenney hasn't heard from you, Nancy," Bess declared. "Maybe she's coming here for a report. Did your dad give her your address?"

"I guess he must have. I'm sorry I haven't better news for her." Nancy sighed. "Perhaps I will have soon."

The girls helped tidy the kitchen. Then Mrs. Glick, the children, Bess, and George went to weed the vegetable patch. Nancy asked to be excused to look around the property. She hoped to find the footprints of the person who had painted the hex symbol.

After figuring out which footprints belonged to the Glicks and her friends, Nancy found an unfamiliar set that led from the barn across a field. She followed them until they came to a road and disappeared. Disappointed, the girl returned to the farm, wanting to be ready to greet the company her father had mentioned.

After lunch Bess disappeared and returned, wearing an attractive blue dress. Mrs. Glick smiled. "You must be expecting a young man."

Bess blushed. "You never can tell," she said, peering out the window. "I had a hunch—and I was right!"

Pulling to a stop in the Glicks' driveway were Nancy's friend Ned Nickerson, Burt Eddleton, who often dated George, and Bess's friend Dave Evans! Delighted, the three girls hurried outside to greet the boys.

"Surprise!" Ned exclaimed.

"Hi!" the other boys greeted the girls.

"This certainly is a surprise, and a grand one," Nancy said. "You're just in time to help us solve a mystery," she added.

"That's what we're here for," said tall, athletic, and brown-haired Ned. "Your dad told me a little about the case. Too bad I was away when it started."

Nancy smiled. "I can sure use a man's help. I hope you've brought us some luck."

"We sure have!"

"We'll all cooperate," said Burt, who was blond and a little shorter and heavier than Ned.

The group went into the house and Nancy presented the boys to Mrs. Glick. At once she insisted that the new visitors stay there. Ned thanked her and accepted.

"Wait until you taste Mrs. Glick's cooking," George remarked to Dave, a rangy, dark-haired young man with green eyes. "You boys will have to go into training to make the football team after you leave here."

Mrs. Glick promised to prepare a special supper in honor of the boys. She refused any assistance from the girls, suggesting that they take their friends on a tour of the countryside.

"Then later you can attend one of the gatherings," she told them. "Over at the Stoltz farm they're having a sing right after supper. Or maybe you would prefer the barn dance at Fischers'."

They all voted for the barn dance, then left on their tour of the area. As the group drove about, Ned became interested in the Amish carriages that passed by.

"Suppose we two go to the barn dance in one of them," he suggested to Nancy.

"Sounds like fun," his date replied, "but we'll have to use an open-top buggy."

"Why?" Ned asked curiously.

"Because all unmarried couples travel that way," she informed him. "The closed carriages are used after the wedding."

Ned whistled. "I'll buy one of those closed jobs after I graduate. How about it, Nancy?"

She pretended not to understand and said, "You'll have to give up college and all worldly pleasures if you expect to marry an Amish girl."

"Oh, aren't you funny!" Ned remarked.

Everyone laughed, but then they became serious as Nancy told them all that had happened since she had left River Heights.

Ned looked grim. "I'm glad we're here. Hoelt's next move may bring you real trouble." Burt and Dave agreed.

By dinnertime, however, the group forgot mystery-solving as they enjoyed a sumptuous meal and prepared for the dance. When a young Amish lad delivered the horse and buggy Ned had ordered, the boys went to inspect them.

"Look, there's a hex sign on the seat," Dave mentioned.

"Better not show Nancy," Ned suggested.

Meanwhile, the girls had come out, and Bess, George, and their escorts left for the dance in Ned's car. Ned helped Nancy into the left side of the buggy, then went around and climbed into the driver's seat. The horse started off at a fast gallop.

It was a cloudy evening and they had not gone more than half a mile before darkness settled. Ned stopped, got out, and turned on the buggy's lanterns.

As they started up again, the horse broke into a brisk trot. Suddenly, the young couple heard the sound of galloping hoofs behind them. Turning around, they saw two buggies, evidently racing. The drivers seemed to be paying no attention to the buggy ahead of them.

Ned pulled as far over to the right side of the road as he could. Apparently neither of the rash young drivers behind him was willing to let the other win. Neck and neck, the racers tried to pass Ned's buggy.

The next moment, the wheels of the nearest

vehicle scraped against those of Nancy and Ned's carriage. Frightened, their horse bolted!

The buggy turned over and Nancy and Ned were thrown out!

Twenty minutes before the accident, Bess, Dave, George, and Burt had reached the dance. The young Amish people who had gathered in the barn were very friendly and welcomed the visitors warmly. The atmosphere was most festive.

Lanterns hung from the rafters, shedding a soft glow over the dancers. The music was very lively and the dances, called by a tall young man, were fast.

After watching several figures of the square dance being performed, Bess and Dave swung into one of the circling groups. George and Burt joined hands with another.

When the music stopped some time later, the four met in a corner of the barn. George remarked, "It's strange that Nancy and Ned haven't arrived yet. But maybe their horse is extra slow."

The words were scarcely out of her mouth when an Amish couple rushed excitedly into the barn. They began to speak rapidly in dialect, flinging their arms about as if describing something they had seen.

Curious, George approached an Amish girl standing near her. "What are they saying?" she asked.

Nancy and Ned were thrown out of the buggy.

"There was a bad accident," the girl replied. "The witch girl was in it!"

Bess and George glanced at each other and hurried toward the couple who had just arrived. They were afraid that the accident referred to involved Nancy and Ned.

"Please tell us in English what happened!" Bess begged the young woman.

"The witch girl—she flew into the air!"

The Amish girl went on to say that her younger brother had been racing with the carriage in which she was riding when they saw a couple in a buggy ahead of them. There was no time to slow down, and as they passed, their vehicle had scraped the wheels of the other carriage. It had overturned, and the couple had seemed to fly out of it!

George was impatient. "What made you call her a witch girl?"

"Because she disappeared," the Amish girl replied in an awed tone. "After the accident, we stopped and went back and looked in the field where the couple were thrown. They were not there!"

"Oh, it must have been Nancy and Ned. They would surely have been here by now if something hadn't happened!" Bess wailed.

George, Bess, Burt, and Dave decided that they must go to the scene of the accident at once. After asking directions, the four hurried off in their car to the field where Nancy and Ned were reported to have disappeared. The open buggy was there, still overturned, but nothing else was in sight.

"My guess is that Nancy and Ned weren't badly hurt," Burt said. "Perhaps the horse ran off and they went to look for him."

Dave agreed and added, "Maybe they returned to Glicks' to report the accident."

The group drove to their host's home, but when they arrived they were told that Nancy and Ned had not come back. Alarmed, Mr. Glick contacted the hospital, but the admitting clerk reported that neither Nancy Drew nor Ned Nickerson had come in for treatment.

"Maybe the police came by and picked them up in a patrol car," Mrs. Glick suggested. They all waited anxiously as her husband got in touch with the police. They knew nothing about the accident but said they would investigate immediately.

"What could have happened to them?" Bess asked.

"Perhaps Nancy and Ned stopped somewhere to freshen up." Burt spoke up. "Right now I bet they're having a good time at the square dance!"

"Good thinking!" George exclaimed. "Let's go back and find out."

After telling the Glicks that they would let them know the outcome, the four young people drove to the Fischer farm. They rushed into the building.

Inside, Bess stepped onto a bench along the wall so that she could look over the dancers' heads. Every couple on the floor was Amish and Nancy and Ned were nowhere in sight!

"Oh, Dave!" she cried, looking down at her date. "What will we do?"

CHAPTER XI

The Vanished Driver

AT this very moment about three miles away the missing couple were on a sleuthing mission. Nancy and Ned were astride the horse he had hired for the evening. They were riding along a lonely road in complete darkness. The animal still wore its blinders. Nancy, seated in front of Ned, held the reins firmly.

A short distance ahead of the unsaddled horse and its two riders was an Amish carriage being pulled by a black horse. The couple were trailing it, hoping their horse's hoofbeats were not being heard.

Ned leaned forward and whispered into Nancy's ear, "You're sure that's the stolen carriage with some of Mrs. Follett's missing furniture in it?"

"I'm almost positive," Nancy said softly.

"And you feel well enough to go on," Ned

asked her solicitously. "Not faint or anything?"

Nancy assured him she was fine. "I can't miss this chance to nab Roger Hoelt!"

Suddenly the carriage they were following turned into a wooded road.

"This may be a trick," Nancy warned, "if the driver knows we're following him."

The girl pulled gently on the reins to slow the horse's gait. Meanwhile, the carriage ahead stopped and its driver got out. Nancy reined in their mount, turning him into the woods.

From among the trees, she and Ned could see a moving light along the road. Was the driver looking for them? As the light played about the nearby area, the hidden couple hardly dared to breathe. Nancy patted the horse soothingly to keep him from pawing the ground or making any sound.

In a few minutes the man turned, retraced his steps, got back in his carriage, and rode off. Nancy and Ned took up the trail again, hoping the hoofbeats of the man's horse would drown out those of their mount.

"I'm sure that fellow knows he's being followed," Nancy said. "We'd better watch out. He may try to trap us!"

Just then the man's horse began to gallop and the carriage swayed from side to side. Nancy and Ned expected it to turn over at any moment.

"That fellow must be crazy to drive so fast," Ned said, "or else he's trying to lose us."

He nudged their horse and it began to run, bringing them closer. After a chase of a quarter of a mile, the carriage stopped abruptly, blocked by a stream. The vehicle swayed a moment but did not go over.

"You stay here," Ned ordered, sliding off the horse. "I'll go ahead and find out what's going on."

Nancy insisted upon following Ned. After securing the horse's reins to a tree trunk, they tiptoed forward, hidden in the shadows of the trees. In a few minutes they reached the carriage.

No one was in it!

"Where did the driver go?" Ned said softly.

Nancy was listening to detect any sound in the nearby woods that might indicate where the man was. She could hear nothing but the chirping of crickets.

"Ned," she whispered, "will you stand guard while I examine the furniture in the carriage? I want to be sure it's part of the Follett collection."

"Go ahead," he urged.

The pieces of furniture were small, and Nancy lifted them out of the vehicle and carried them, one by one, to the carriage lamps to look them over. Each resembled items on Mrs. Tenney's list, but there was no way to identify them positively as the stolen articles.

Disappointed, Nancy had returned all but one piece, which she now examined. It was a small hassock with mahogany legs and a petit-point top with a design of red roses and festoons of green leaves. It fitted the description of a footstool taken from the Follett mansion!

"Ned," Nancy whispered, excited. "We're surely on the right track. This is exactly like one of the stolen pieces on the inventory. And this horse is black, like the one Hoelt took. I think we have enough evidence to report him to the police."

"Great!" Ned exclaimed, but he reminded her that by the time they could get to a phone, the thief might return and drive away with the evidence.

Nancy nodded. "You're right. Then we'll have to take the horse and carriage with us!" she declared. "You ride the horse and I'll drive the buggy."

Ned did not think this was a safe thing for Nancy to do. The man who had been driving the carriage might be waiting in ambush and would prevent them from reporting the incident to the police.

"That could be," Nancy said, "but I think he's not very familiar with this area. He didn't know about the stream and when he reached it, he was afraid to cross over."

Ned said that sounded logical, and added that the man probably had known someone was on his trail and had fled in fear of being caught. The question was, Where was he now?

Nancy got into the carriage and urged the horse into a full turn. Then, leading the way, she started off with Ned guarding the rear.

Though both the young people had shown no fear of what they were about to do, each of them was nervous. It was possible that the missing driver had gone off for reinforcements.

At any moment Roger Hoelt and his assistants might come to claim what they considered to be their property! What they might do to the young couple to keep them from going to the police gave Nancy and Ned some uneasy moments. But as they reached the end of the woods road, the tension began to lessen. The riders were not stopped. In fact, they met no one on the road.

Since Nancy knew none of the farmers in the neighborhood and saw no lights in the houses they passed, she decided it would be unwise to stop to telephone at any of them. She concluded that the best plan would be to go to the dance.

Half an hour later she and Ned reached the Fischers'. Instead of going to the barn, where the dance was still in progress, Nancy drove directly to the house. By the time the door was opened by a smiling, broad-shouldered man, Ned had joined her.

Mr. Fischer invited them into the kitchen. Together, they quickly told their story, and the Amish man's face showed his astonishment. He immediately called the State Police.

"They will send a man," he reported after he had talked with the captain. "It is good that you two found the stolen furniture. But it is too bad that you should miss the dance. Why don't you go over there and make a square? I will call you when the police come."

Nancy thanked him, but said that after their accident she was more ready for a bottle of liniment than a dance!

"I guess I'm not so hardy as your Amish girls," she added.

The man chuckled. He remarked diplomatically that even an Amish girl who had been thrown out of a buggy and then ridden an unsaddled horse for miles might need a massage with liniment. He offered to awaken his wife to give Nancy a rubdown, but she said a hot bath and a good night's sleep would fix her up.

While waiting for the police to arrive, she and Ned talked to Mr. Fischer about the farms in the vicinity, and Nancy asked him if he had ever heard of a place called the *schnitz*.

"No," the man said. "But I have not lived here many years. I came from Ohio."

At once Nancy inquired if he had ever heard of Roger Hoelt from Ohio. The farmer shook his head.

At this moment a car stopped at the house and two State Police officers came in. They introduced themselves as Officers Wagner and Schmidt.

"You are the couple who may have found some stolen furniture?" Officer Wagner asked Nancy and Ned.

"And a stolen horse and carriage," Ned added.

Nancy told the police about her interview at the carriage factory, and also of hearing that a black horse had disappeared from one of the nearby farms. Officer Schmidt pulled a little book from his pocket and turned several pages.

"Here is a report on both items," he said. "And unless the person who stole the carriage added a final coat of paint to the underside of the right shaft, it may be possible for us to identify the carriage."

The group walked outside. Officer Schmidt took a flashlight from his pocket, got down on the ground, and beamed the light under the right shaft. A smile crossed his face.

"This is it, all right," he said. "The final coat was never put on."

Both officers congratulated Nancy and Ned on

recovering the stolen carriage, then looked into the back of it.

"What makes you think this is part of the collection of stolen furniture?" Officer Wagner asked Nancy.

She told him about the petit-point pattern on the hassock. He smiled and remarked that she certainly was a thorough and discerning detective.

"We'll take the horse, carriage, and furniture with us," said Officer Wagner, "and would you like us to return the horse and buggy you rented?"

"Yes, thank you," Ned said, and told the policemen where they would find the carriage.

The officers said they would explain what had happened to the owner. Ned asked them to have the man send him a bill and gave his address.

After the police had gone, Nancy and Ned decided to go to the dance and find their friends. They went outside, and for the first time realized that Ned's car was not there. They concluded that their friends must have gone back to the Glicks'.

"But how are we going to get home?" Nancy asked.

"Surely somebody here will give us a lift," Ned suggested.

They walked to the barn door and stepped

inside. They had no sooner appeared than one of the Amish girls who was dancing stopped short and shrieked.

Pointing a finger at the couple, she cried out, "The witch girl! The witch boy! They've flown back here to hex us!"

The dancing ceased abruptly and the musicians stopped playing. There was a surge of unfriendly looking young men and women toward Nancy and Ned. Fearfully the couple wondered what was going to happen!

CHAPTER XII

A Hideout

WEARY from the experiences of the evening, Nancy was in no condition to cope with the on-coming hostile group. But Ned instantly took command of the situation.

"Stop!" he cried, holding up his hands.

As the young Amish couples paused, he told them that all the talk about the witch girl and boy was utterly ridiculous. Furthermore, both he and Nancy might have lost their lives because of the foolishness of one of their drivers.

There was silence for a moment, then one of the boys called out, "*Ya*, but I go by the old ideas. This girl makes trouble, ain't?"

"On the contrary," Ned said in a loud voice so that all could hear him. "Nancy Drew is doing your neighborhood a favor. She has just found a horse and a carriage that was stolen from some of your people."

The dancers exchanged glances of amazement. The girl who had made the original statement about Nancy being a witch girl withdrew from the forefront of the group, embarrassed. Ned went on to tell the whole story.

"Nancy is an excellent detective," he stated firmly in conclusion, "but she is not a witch girl. And now, tell us where our friends are. We would like to go home."

Some of the people in the group shook their heads, then most of them turned away. The music started and the dancing began again, but several young men approached Nancy and Ned and offered to drive them wherever they wanted to go.

"I am sorry about what happened," one of them said. "We thank you for what you have done."

Ned was about to accept the offer of a lift when he and Nancy heard the sound of a familiar car motor. Looking outside, they saw Ned's convertible come to a stop. Bess and George, spotting the missing couple, quickly climbed out and rushed over to them.

"Oh, I'm so glad you're all right!" Bess exclaimed, hugging Nancy.

George added, "You scared us out of our wits. We heard you had an accident, and we saw the overturned buggy. We couldn't find you."

"We'll tell you all about it on the way home," Nancy said, as Ned took her arm and helped her into the car.

Burt and Dave grinned. "Why didn't you two tell us you were going to ride around all of Lancaster County by yourselves on a horse?"

"How were we to know?" Ned joked.

As they rode toward the Glick farm, Nancy surprised the others by saying that she and Ned had actually come to the dance hours before.

"You heard about our little accident," she said. "Well, Ned and I chased the horse and caught him. We were so close to the dance that we thought we'd just ride him there and make arrangements to pick up the carriage later.

"After we tethered the horse and were walking to the barn, we noticed an Amish carriage and a black horse some distance away from the others. My curiosity got the better of me and I decided to take a look. No one was in the carriage, but in the back was some furniture that looked like the stolen Follett pieces."

"What!" Bess and George cried in unison.

Nancy smiled. "At least I thought so, and later I found out I was right. Well, we waited around to see if Roger Hoelt was in the vicinity. In a few minutes a man came sneaking around the side of the barn, as if he had been spying on the dancers."

"I guess he was looking for you, Nancy," Burt put in. "Was he Roger Hoelt?"

"No. The man came to the carriage, got in, and drove off."

Ned chuckled. "And you know Nancy!" he

said. "She decided he was a pal of Hoelt's. And of course she wanted to follow him. So we did!"

He told the rest of the story and the others listened in amazement.

Upon reaching the Glicks', they found that the cobbler and his wife were still up. The couple were overjoyed to see Nancy and Ned and insisted on hearing the whole story.

When it was finished, Mrs. Glick said, "How good that you are safe. And you must be hungry. We will have a little bite to eat. You will all sleep better."

As she started toward the stove, Mr. Glick raised his hand. "That is good, Mama," he said. "But first, we will say a prayer of thanks for the safe return of our guests."

The group bowed their heads and he said a short prayer in German. At its conclusion everyone kept his head bowed in silence for nearly a minute. Each, in his own words, added a personal thanks for the safe return of Nancy and Ned. Then, after they had all eaten a hearty midnight snack, everyone went to bed.

After breakfast the following morning, the boys announced that they must leave for their summer jobs. Each declared that he had crowded a lot of fun and excitement into the short visit.

"I'm sorry you can't stay long enough to solve the whole mystery, Ned," Nancy said. "You've been a big help."

After the girls had waved good-by to the boys

from the lane, they went into the house to help Mrs. Glick with the household chores. As they worked, Nancy remarked that she wanted to start out soon and continue the search for Roger Hoelt.

Mrs. Glick's face fell. "I was hoping you would go to Mrs. Stoltz's quilting with me," she said. "It is for her daughter."

When Nancy asked her about the "quilting," Mrs. Glick explained that an Amish woman spends many years before her marriage making articles for her new home.

"You mean that they know ahead of time whom they are going to marry?" Bess asked, wide-eyed.

The woman laughed. "Oh, no," she said. "But Amish people like to be ready for the future. After a girl is asked in marriage, it is not long before the wedding takes place. She has to have her dowry ready." Mrs. Glick looked steadfastly at the three girls. "Have you made no preparations for your weddings?"

The girls blushed scarlet and confessed that they had not even thought of a dowry. Mrs. Glick shook her head sadly. "You should not stay *leddich* too long," she said.

Noting her listeners' puzzled expressions, she translated, "That means not married. Ned, Burt, and Dave are such nice *yuung maane*."

"Yes," said Bess, "they are nice young men, but none of us is ready to marry yet."

"You are old enough," Mrs. Glick insisted.

"You should think about it. Anyway, I want you to go to the quilting with me. You will see what an Amish girl does so that she will have many things ready for her new home."

The girls thought it would be interesting. They said they would stay at the quilting for a little while, then go on their sleuthing trip. An hour later they set off for the Stoltz farmhouse. Mrs. Glick drove her own car and the girls went in Nancy's convertible.

At the Stoltz house they found that several women from neighboring farms had gathered in the parlor. It was explained to the visitors that these were friends and relatives of the family and that they were going to help sixteen-year-old Rebecca Stoltz make a fancy bedspread.

A large wooden quilting frame had been set up. Stretched taut across it was a white muslin bedspread. Rebecca had just finished cutting out pieces of colored cloth for the pattern to be sewed on the spread. Later, it would be quilted.

Around the edges of the spread was to be a diamond design in bright blue. The center section would be covered at intervals by big red tulips with green stems and leaves growing out of terra-cotta flowerpots.

Four young women had seated themselves around the quilting frame, threaded needles in hand. Quickly they began to stitch on the blue diamonds Rebecca handed them.

Nancy, Bess, and George were amazed at the dexterity of the sewers. Not a stitch showed!

The girls stayed for half an hour. Rebecca showed them her dowry, which she kept in an old cedar chest. It held several dozen embroidered pillowcases, dresser scarfs, towels, sheets, and another bright quilt.

Finally, when Nancy told her she and her friends must be on their way, Rebecca said she would like to give her guests something to remind them of the Amish quilting party. She lifted out a large pillowcase filled with pieces of material of various colors and designs, and gave a large handful of them to each girl.

"You will your own quilt begin, ain't?" she asked, smiling.

Nancy and her friends promised to do this. "We will start patchwork quilts with these," Bess said, and Rebecca nodded contentedly.

After thanking her and saying good-by to Mrs. Glick and the others, the three girls left the house. As they started off in the car, George asked, "Where are we going, Nancy?"

The young detective said she thought that the man who had run away from the carriage the night before had started toward the Hoelts' hiding place. When the driver had realized he was being followed, he had deliberately taken another route.

"What I'm going to try to do," said Nancy, "is

figure out at which point he turned off from the direction leading to his destination."

Bess asked Nancy if she had any idea where this was. "I think it may be where the man turned right into the wooded road," the young sleuth answered. "When I reach that point, I'll go in the opposite direction."

Driving to the spot, she pulled to the left and followed a narrow road for about two miles. Here it became little more than a footpath. Nancy drove along for a short distance, then decided it was too rough for further progress in the convertible.

"I'm going to park in this field," she said, "and we'll continue on foot."

The path they followed became more and more overgrown and finally ended at a woods.

"Well, this didn't turn out so well," George remarked, as the three peered ahead into the tangled undergrowth.

"The wilder it gets, the more likely it is to be Roger Hoelt's hideout," Nancy reminded her. "Let's go on."

She set off through the woods with determination, the cousins following. After they had tramped a quarter of a mile they came to a clearing. Through the trees the girls could see a tumble-down house at one side of it.

"We'd better be careful," Bess warned.

The girls proceeded cautiously. They spread

out, with Nancy in the middle, their eyes on the house. Suddenly George gasped "Oh!" as her right foot sank into a hole.

A second later, as she tried to wrench her foot free, George found she could not do it. Her whole right leg sank lower.

The next second, the earth caved in around her and she went down with it!

CHAPTER XIII

The Attic's Secret

"HELP! I'll be smothered!" George called out.
The terrified girl was sinking lower and lower
into the hole.

Thoroughly alarmed, Nancy and Bess hurried
toward George, but stopped a short distance
away.

"Careful, Bess," Nancy warned. "We can't help
George if we fall in too. Some of this other
ground may be treacherous."

The two girls tested the ground before taking
each step. Meanwhile, George kept giving urgent
cries, for she had now sunk up to her waist in
the earth. The more she struggled, the deeper
she went!

"Try to keep calm, George!" Nancy cried.
"We'll get you out in a minute!" She turned to
her other friend. "Bess," she directed, "lie down
on the ground behind me."

While Bess did this, Nancy quickly stretched out full length on her stomach at the edge of the hole. She reached out toward George.

"Grab my ankles, Bess!" she called again. "When I count three, start wriggling backward."

Taking hold of George's wrists, Nancy said, "Lock your hands over my wrists. Ready! One, two, three!"

Instantly, Bess began squirming backward across the ground. Nancy did the same. But their efforts accomplished little to free George.

"Pull a little harder, Bess," Nancy called.

Bess glanced backward. Almost directly behind her was a small tree. She hooked one ankle around it to give her better leverage. When she and Nancy tried a second time, they were able to heave George a foot out of the pit!

The girls rested briefly, then repeated the operation. A few more tugs and George was free, sprawled on the ground, a safe distance beyond the edge of the hole. A moment later the earth on both sides of the hole fell away.

"Good night!" she shuddered. "You were just in time. What a close call!"

"What could have caused the cave-in?" Bess asked.

"I think there may have been a sluiceway here long ago," Nancy declared. "Probably at this point there was a water wheel and a little dam.

It has partially filled in, but the water keeps the ground above it soft."

Nancy went on thoughtfully, "Since nobody came out of the house when you cried for help, George, it must be deserted. Let's find out!"

The others nodded and the three advanced cautiously toward the one-story dwelling. When they reached it, Nancy knocked on the door. There was no reply and finally she turned the knob. To her surprise, it opened easily and the young sleuth led the way inside. All was quiet.

"I doubt that anyone is here," said George, as the friends wandered from room to room, noting that not one had a piece of furniture.

Finally they reached the kitchen, which did not even contain a stove. Nancy pointed out a trap door leading to an attic. They were about to turn away when suddenly they heard a thud overhead.

Nancy put her fingers to her lips, and the girls stood in complete silence. The sound was not repeated as they gazed steadily above them.

Finally George whispered, "I guess it was nothing."

Nancy shook her head and again put a finger to her lips. Pointing upward, she indicated that she was going to investigate the attic.

She motioned for Bess to bend down. The plump girl groaned as Nancy climbed on her shoulders, reached upward, and tilted the trap door open.

The next second a shower of dusty newspapers dropped down. Nancy lost her balance and fell to the floor. Bess was bowled over, her eyes full of dirt. Almost at the same instant, a heavy bundle of papers landed squarely on George!

The room was a cloud of dust. Coughing and choking, the three girls ran to the front door. After clearing their lungs outdoors, Bess and George asked Nancy if she had hurt herself in the fall.

"Not much," Nancy replied, "but I don't believe those papers tumbled down by themselves."

Bess became alarmed. "You mean someone was in the attic and pushed them down on us?"

"Yes, I do," Nancy said. "Come on. We're going to find out who it was!"

When the girls returned to the kitchen, they saw that the back door was open. Also, someone had jumped down from the attic. Footprints were evident in the heavy dust.

"They lead out the door!" George cried.

"I'm going to follow them," Nancy said tensely. "Bess, you come with me. George, will you stay here as guard?"

"Sure."

As Nancy and Bess ran through the rear exit, George fixed her eyes on the trap door, wonder-

A shower of dusty newspapers poured down.

ing uneasily if there could be a second person in the attic. She decided to find out.

Going to the front door, George slammed it hard, then tiptoed back, peeking around the door to the kitchen. She waited for several minutes but no one appeared in the trap-door opening.

At last George went outside. She walked around the house, but found nothing suspicious. The girl's attention was suddenly arrested by a gnarled old cherry tree in the nearby woods. From its limbs hung rows of a parasitic whiplike growth, giving the tree a grotesque appearance. Several branches crossed so that they resembled a witch on a broom.

"A witch tree!" George exclaimed.

As she stared at the tree, the girl became convinced it must have something to do with the hex symbol.

Suddenly a woman's shrill scream split the silence. George turned in the direction from which it had come, but could see no one. She paused.

The scream might mean that George's friends needed help, or it might have been uttered by someone else as a ruse to get her away from the old house. She decided to stand her ground.

A few moments later Nancy and Bess emerged from among the trees. George asked if either of them had screamed.

"No," Nancy replied. "That was an Amish woman we saw in the woods. For no apparent reason, she screamed and ran off as fast as she could."

Bess continued, "We decided she was probably some farm girl picking berries or wild flowers. Maybe a noise in the underbrush startled her."

"Did you discover anything?" George asked.

"No," Nancy answered. "We couldn't find any trail or clues in this wooded area so we decided to turn back. Any more visitors?"

George shook her head. "But see what I found," she said, pointing to the twisted old cherry tree. "Doesn't it look like a witch tree?"

"It sure does," Nancy said, and ran over to inspect it. She searched the crotches of the low branches, but found nothing unusual on or near the tree.

"If it's tied up with the witch tree symbol and Hoelt," she said thoughtfully, "it could be a landmark for directions to the *schnitz*. I'm going to investigate the attic for any clues to the identity of the person who was up there, or to the witch tree symbol."

Once more the girls returned to the house. Again Bess bent over so that Nancy might pull herself up through the trap-door opening.

"Here, take my pocket flashlight," George offered as Nancy peered into the dark opening.

"Thanks."

Nimbly, the slim girl hoisted herself into the small attic. Beaming the flashlight about, for a

moment Nancy saw nothing. Then her alert eyes
picked out a dust-covered object shoved far back
under the eaves. She crawled over to it.

Nancy brushed off a layer of dirt from the article and discovered that it was an old German
Bible about ten by twelve inches in size. Its cover
was brittle and frayed.

Picking it up gently, Nancy returned to the
trap door. "Bess, will you please take this?" she
requested. "And be careful with it."

Getting on her knees, Nancy held on to the
edge of the opening with one hand, and with the
other she passed the Bible to Bess. Then she
lightly swung herself downward and jumped to
the floor.

The girls hastened to examine the old book.
The flyleaf was speckled with brown from age.
Nancy, noticing some faded writing in ink, shone
her light on the page, and read aloud, " 'Given
to Rachel Hoelt by her parents at the time of
her marriage.' "

"Hypers!" George exclaimed. "Do you suppose
this house is still owned by the Hoelt family?"

"If it were," Nancy said, "I think the police
would have looked here for Roger Hoelt."

Bess thought the crook might have known the
house was empty and used it as a hiding place,
but Nancy pointed out it contained none of the
stolen furniture that was missing from the carriage she and Ned had recovered.

"Also," she reasoned, "Roger Hoelt uses both an automobile and a horse and buggy. He couldn't drive either of them in here. Besides, this house shows no signs of recent occupancy."

"I agree," said George, "but the witch tree could be a signpost. We'll keep on looking."

Nancy agreed and also felt they should take the old Bible with them and leave it at the Glicks' for safekeeping. Later, she would search for law-abiding members of the Hoelt family who might be interested in preserving this valuable find.

"I think Roger Hoelt probably was the person we surprised in the attic," Bess now declared. "Maybe he was looking for this book and we interrupted his search."

They wrapped the Bible carefully in some of the old newspapers and carried it to the car.

"I have a hunch that we may be narrowing our search for Roger Hoelt and Manda Kreutz," she announced as they drove away.

"By now, Manda may be back home," George mused, thinking that the Amish girl might have found out the Hoelts' true aims and character.

"Perhaps," said Nancy doubtfully. "But I think we would have heard of it through the grapevine if she had returned to her family. Later we can stop at the Kreutz farm and see."

By the time they got back to the Glick home, Mrs. Glick had returned from the quilting party. She was bustling about, preparing dinner.

"Something smells mighty good!" George smiled.

Mrs. Glick wiped her hands on her apron. "We are having 'old shoes' and *milich flitche.* 'Old shoes' are mashed potatoes inside of a dumpling. The *milich flitche* is pie," she went on, "made of flour, cream, sugar, and cinnamon."

During the delicious meal the girls told of their day's experiences, and asked if Mrs. Glick could explain the odd-looking tree they had seen.

The woman nodded. "It has *hex bayse* growing on its branches. That means witch's broom."

This information made the girls feel even more sure that at last they were on the right track. They told the Glicks of their plan to call on the Kreutzes to see if Manda had returned.

"I'm sure that if she had," Mrs. Glick said, "the women at the quilting party would have known about it. One of them did say that the Kreutzes think you're responsible for Manda's vanishing."

"That's why they acted so peculiarly!" Nancy exclaimed, recalling the couple's strange actions.

"Maybe they decided we had encouraged Manda to learn more about life away from the farm," Bess said.

Despite this, Nancy and Bess left for the Kreutz homestead after dinner. George remained behind, since her ankle was throbbing a bit.

"If Manda isn't here," Bess said, "I'd hate to

have Papa Kreutz go into a rage again when we arrive."

Nancy grinned at this remark as she drove up the lane to the farm. She parked, then walked with Bess to the door of the house. Bess was about to knock when the door was opened by Mrs. Kreutz.

The woman grabbed each girl by a shoulder and yanked her inside crying, *"Dummel dich!"*

CHAPTER XIV

A Groeszdawdi Clue

Mrs. Kreutz quickly closed the kitchen door behind Nancy and Bess, and said, "Please to forgive me for speaking Pennsylvania Dutch to you. I was saying 'hurry'!"

"What's the matter?" Bess asked quickly.

Manda's mother looked around as if afraid someone would hear her reply. In a whisper she said, "I could not let you stay outdoors. Papa has come to believe you girls persuaded Manda to run away. He has told many people this. If he should drive in now, please run yourselves the front door out."

Nancy felt that she should remind Mrs. Kreutz that the convertible parked outside was a dead giveaway. But before she could say a word, Mrs. Kreutz asked breathlessly, "Have you news of Manda?"

"We were hoping she might have returned

home," Nancy replied. "We haven't been able to find her."

Mrs. Kreutz wrung her hands. "Oh, my little daughter!" she wailed. "If it had not been for Papa saying no one could talk to her, she would be here now. I am so afraid she is in danger."

The girls agreed with this but did not voice their opinion. Instead, they assured Mrs. Kreutz that they were doing everything possible to find Manda.

"The police are trying to locate Mr. and Mrs. Hoelt, the people we think Manda is working for," Bess added.

Nancy brought the girl's mother up-to-date on all that had happened, ending with the question, "The man on the street who spoke to Manda's cousin Melinda, said, 'Get to the *schnitz!*' Have you any idea what he meant?"

When Mrs. Kreutz said no, Nancy asked whether the woman had ever heard of a storehouse for dried apples in the neighborhood. At this remark Mrs. Kreutz turned pale. Grasping Nancy's hand, she said, "Manda asked me that very question!"

"I believe that's where she has gone," Nancy said. "Where is the storehouse?"

Sadly the Amish woman admitted that she did not know. She had never heard of such a place.

"If Manda was trying to find it," said Nancy,

"where would she go to get information about it?"

Mrs. Kreutz replied that there was one very old man in the neighborhood who might be able to help. "He knows about everything that took place long ago," she said. "I have never heard of any new storehouses, so this place must have been used years ago."

"Who is this man and where does he live?" Nancy asked eagerly.

"He's Groeszdawdi Esch," Mrs. Kreutz answered. "He lives in one end of a three-generation house."

Bess wanted to know what this was, and Mrs. Kreutz explained that in Amish country, families rarely separate. Sometimes a man will build a house on part of his property for a son about to be married. "Other parents," she said, "build a wing onto the main house, and the father and mother move into it when one of the sons marries."

"And where does the third house come in?" Bess asked.

Mrs. Kreutz said it was hard to explain this in English. Anyway, there were three houses attached, each smaller than the one beside it. In the smallest house lived the grandfather, in the center building was the father, and in the largest house was the grandson and his family.

"Groeszdawdi Esch lives in the smallest house,"

she said. Pointing in a northwesterly direction,
she added, "If you could fly like a crow, you
would hit on it."

"I'm sure we can find it," Nancy said. "And
now we had better go before your husband re-
turns."

Mrs. Kreutz said yes. He had gone to a cow
sale to sell the ugly bull that had attacked him,
but he probably would be home any minute. The
girls hurried outside, climbed into the car, and
drove off.

They found the Esch farm with little trouble.
As they reached the barn they were surprised to
see a dozen Amish carriages assembled. "There
must be a party going on," Nancy said.

At that moment a young boy carrying a bucket
of apple parings dashed out of a small stone building. He dumped the contents of the pail into the
pigsty.

"I'll bet this is an apple *schnitzing*," Bess remarked.

Realizing that Groeszdawdi Esch and everyone
else on the farm would be in the kettle house,
Nancy and Bess got out of the car and went directly there.

"Doesn't it smell heavenly!" said Bess as she
sniffed the spicy aroma coming from the building.

Nancy and Bess stepped inside and watched
the busy scene with fascination. Seated on chairs
and apple crates were several men and women,

old and young. Each one held a metal, box-shaped apple parer on his lap. It worked with a quick turn of the handle and rapidly took the skin off the apple. Next, the fruit was cored and put into large kettles, which were lifted into a warm oven. Here the moisture would be baked out.

Several minutes passed before the girls were noticed. Then a young woman left her work and came over to ask if she could be of assistance to them. Nancy stated that she had come to talk to Groeszdawdi Esch.

"I will get him," the woman offered.

Presently an elderly man with snow-white hair and beard approached them. He had kindly blue eyes, and despite his advanced age was tall and erect.

The old man smiled pleasantly at the visitors. "Groeszdawdi can help you?" he asked.

Nancy explained that she was looking for a place known as the *schnitz,* which she thought was an old-time dried-apple storehouse.

"*Ach, ya,*" the man said. "I know the place. A long time ago it belonged to a farmer named Hoelt."

Nancy could hardly conceal her excitement. "Yes, go on," she urged.

"The Hoelts have not lived there for a long time," Groeszdawdi went on. "They sold the place to city people named Fuller. But now they have abandoned it."

"Why?" Bess spoke up.

Groeszdawdi Esch looked first at one girl, then the other. "Before I tell you, explain why you want to know about it."

Nancy wondered what was behind the elderly man's question, but she replied that Manda Kreutz was missing, and that she thought Manda might be hiding at the *schnitz*.

"*Gfaiirlich! Ess iss wie toedt!*"

The girls waited for Mr. Esch to translate. In a moment he did. "It's dangerous! It's like death!"

He went on to say that if Manda were there, she, too, might vanish mysteriously, as many others had on that farm.

"But why?" Nancy cried. "Tell us so that we can save her!"

Groeszdawdi Esch shook his head and wagged a finger at the girls. "Stay away from that spot! It is bad luck—very bad luck!"

CHAPTER XV

The Gypsy's Story

WOULD Groeszdawdi Esch refuse to tell them where the *schnitz* was? Nancy and Bess wondered. Since he had pronounced it a dangerous place from which people had disappeared, it was unlikely that he would reveal its location.

Nancy, however, finally persuaded him to tell her where the place was. He hesitated a long time, then finally said, "Go four miles north from here. You will see a lane running through a field that has not been tilled for years. The road is overgrown and rutty. Nobody uses it, but you can't miss it if you keep your eyes open."

On a hunch Nancy asked whether there was another house on the property some distance from the main building. Groeszdawdi Esch nodded, saying that the old Hoelt family had several children. The father had built houses for them in several locations on the property.

"Was one of the women named Rachel Hoelt?" Nancy asked.

The old man looked at her searchingly and asked how she happened to know of a Rachel Hoelt, who had died fifty years before. Nancy said that she had seen an old Bible with the name in it.

"That's the farm," he said. "But I'm telling you again, stay away from it!"

"Why is it dangerous?" Bess spoke up.

Groeszdawdi Esch took a deep breath, then began his story. He used so many Pennsylvania Dutch words and phrases with English that it was difficult for the girls to understand him. But after they had questioned him several times, Nancy and Bess finally got the gist of the tale.

A long time ago, the storyteller related, when the Hoelts lived on the farm, some members of their family vanished mysteriously and were never seen again. Neighbors concluded that there was a hex on the family. One day a band of gypsies came along, and they set up their tents on the property.

"Old Mr. Hoelt was furious," Groeszdawdi said. "He was sure the gypsies would bring him even worse luck. He ordered them away, but instead of leaving they only moved to the woods on his property."

It seemed that old Mr. Hoelt was not aware of this, but several of his children went to the encampment and became friendly with the gypsies. One of the women was a beautiful, young fortuneteller. Mr. Hoelt's eldest son and she fell in love and planned to marry.

The old man found out and stopped the marriage by threatening to disinherit his son. The fortuneteller was furious. She told him that she knew the secret of why members of his family had disappeared, but she would never tell him unless he consented to the marriage. It was a terrible choice for the old man to make, but he decided to keep his son at home.

Later, people said that the gypsy woman, out of love for the young man, had left him a clue to the secret. She had written it down in English on a piece of paper and hidden it in a table, which she had left behind for her beloved. According to rumors, this table had somehow been acquired by the gypsies from the collection in George Washington's home.

As Groeszdawdi Esch finished the story, Nancy and Bess glanced at each other. Was this the table Roger Hoelt had been searching for?

Mr. Esch told the girls that the present owner of the property, Mr. Fuller, had also had bad luck on the farm. No one in his family had disappeared, but his cattle had become ill and died, he had had poor crops and several accidents, and illness had hounded the family.

"Who is operating the farm now?" Nancy asked.

"No one," the man replied. "The Fullers have left, but they have not put the property up for sale. I do not know whether they intend to come back."

Nancy concluded that this might explain why Roger Hoelt and his wife had chosen this particular place in which to hide. He was trying to find out what the secret was. Should he discover it, and learn that the answer might bring him a lot of money, he would undoubtedly offer to buy back the property.

A faraway look came into Groeszdawdi's eyes. Then he said, "You say that maybe Manda Kreutz is hiding on the Fuller property?"

"I'm afraid so," Nancy answered. "I'm going to go there and try to find her. Have you any idea what makes the place dangerous, so I could avoid any trouble?"

Groeszdawdi Esch said it was a mystery to him and that he had never heard anything to give him the slightest clue as to what the secret was.

"But the few people who know the story stay away from the place like the plague!" he told them.

Nancy thanked the man for his information and promised to be very careful in her search. He smiled and said he hoped that Manda would be safe at home soon and that her papa would not be too harsh with her.

"Manda is pretty and she is a good worker," he said. "She will soon get a husband and her papa will not have to worry," he added, chuckling.

The girls laughed, recalling that Melinda had said the same thing. They left.

Nancy wanted to start immediately for the Fuller farm, but Bess protested. "Nancy Drew, after all you've heard, you're going to go there?"

"Yes."

"Well, you'll take somebody except just me," she announced firmly. "We'll collect George and half a dozen other people."

Nancy laughed. "Where are we going to get all these people?"

Bess said she did not know, but they were not going alone. The girls continued to discuss the matter as they drove off.

"You're hinting that I call in the police, Bess," said Nancy. "I don't want to do that. We haven't one definite thing to go on. Dragging officers out on what may be a wild-goose chase wouldn't be right.

"What I propose to do is find out whether Mr. and Mrs. Hoelt are really hiding at the Fuller farm. And if Manda is there working for them, I want to get her away before I call the police. We don't want Manda to get any bad publicity."

Bess finally conceded that Nancy was right.
"But it's getting late. I won't hear of your going
until tomorrow morning."

"All right," Nancy agreed.

Presently she remarked that it was likely the
furniture thief and his wife were using Manda as
a front. So far as the Amish girl knew, the couple
were honest.

"Manda has led a sheltered life," said Nancy.
"She would probably believe any story the Hoelts
might tell her and pass it on to any unexpected
visitors."

"Of course the unexpected visitors aren't sup-
posed to include you, George, and me," Bess said.
"Roger Hoelt tried to brain us in that little cabin.
No telling what he'll do if we show up at his real
hideout."

Nancy did not comment on this. Instead, she
said, "I'm convinced now that the woman who
screamed in the woods and ran away was either
Manda or Mrs. Hoelt. With the Amish head
covering, it's hard to distinguish faces from a distance."

Bess looked worried. She suggested that the
secret danger connected with the property might
have caused the woman to scream. "Maybe it's
some kind of a witch or other hex," she murmured.

"It was probably only a snake," said Nancy.

At the Glicks' farm, Nancy and Bess related their latest news. The children and their parents were intrigued.

"What is a gypsy like?" Becky asked. "And how do you tell fortunes?"

Her mother explained, then said, "There is no more sense to fortunetelling than there is to hexing. Now we will talk no more about nonsense."

The visitors took the cue, changed the subject, and later helped Mrs. Glick prepare supper. Glancing outside, Nancy saw Becky and Henner playing in the barnyard.

As she watched, the little boy raised a slingshot. Nancy was amazed that his parents would let him use this dangerous plaything. Henner was very proficient and could make a stone whistle a long distance through the air.

"Henner would make a good hunter," Nancy remarked to the boy's mother. "He has a very accurate aim with his slingshot."

Mrs. Glick agreed, but said that once in a while he became erratic and hit something he had not intended to. "But he is improving every day," she said.

Directly after supper the three girls took a walk and discussed the mystery again. They had just started back to the house when Mrs. Glick called to them.

"Telephone call for you from home, Bess," she said.

Bess hurried into the house. The other girls followed, thinking there might be some news for them too.

As they stepped through the door, Bess was saying, "Hello!" She listened for a few seconds, then hung up.

Suddenly Bess burst into tears!

CHAPTER XVI

A Slingshot Strikes

"Bess, what happened?" Nancy cried, rushing to her friend's side and putting an arm around her. "Is it bad news?"

Bess stopped sobbing and said in a quivering voice, "Nancy, I hate to tell you this, but it was your father's secretary calling. Oh dear, I don't know how to break such news."

Nancy's heart began to pound. "Tell me, whatever it is," she begged.

Finally Bess said that Mr. Drew was dangerously ill in a hospital and it was doubtful that he would recover. "He keeps calling for you all the time, Nancy," Bess went on. "Everybody thinks you should come home at once."

Nancy had turned chalk white. She was completely stunned—too stunned even to shed a tear. Like someone in a trance, she turned toward the stairway, saying she would get her car keys and leave at once. Bess quickly said she would go along.

Mrs. Glick hurried to Nancy's side. Putting a motherly arm around the girl's waist, she told her how sorry she was to hear the bad news.

Mr. Glick had risen from his chair. He also came to Nancy's side to offer his sympathy. "You should not be driving all night," he said. "Anyway, it would be faster for you to fly. I will telephone the airport to see about a plane and drive you over there."

Nancy thanked him, agreeing that would be the best way for her to get to River Heights in a hurry. She hoped she would not be too late to see her father alive.

All this while George had remained silent. It was not because of lack of sympathy, but it had occurred to her that the whole procedure was almost irregular. If Mr. Drew were so ill, Hannah would have returned to River Heights and called Nancy direct. Or, her own or Bess's parents would have been in touch with the girls.

The more George thought about it, the more suspicious she became that the telephone call might have been a hoax. Mr. Drew's secretary was on vacation and a substitute was taking her place. Bess had never spoken to the girl, so she would not have been able to identify the voice. It would be very easy for someone else to pretend to be his secretary.

"Mrs. Glick," said George, "did the operator tell you the call was from River Heights?"

"Why, no," the Amish woman replied. "It was the secretary herself I talked to."

George now told them of her suspicions and suggested that they call the Drew home. If there was no answer, she would try her own house.

Nancy had paused on the stairway. Her heart leaped with hope! George's idea was very good. Nancy prayed the girl was right and that this was a hoax!

Everyone waited breathlessly while George placed the call to the Drew house. There was no answer. Nancy relaxed a little. This must mean that Hannah Gruen was still visiting her sister! But George wasted no time in trying her own home. Less than a minute later she was saying hello to her mother, and adding, "Is it true that Nancy's father is in the hospital and very ill?"

"Why, absolutely not!" Mrs. Fayne answered. "I was speaking with Mr. Drew only five minutes ago. He had returned home from the trip he told Nancy about, but was leaving for another overnight trip."

"Hold the line just a moment, Mother," said George. She turned and relayed the good news to everyone. Nancy's eyes filled with tears of joy and relief. She was sorry not to have spoken with her father. He had probably just missed the telephone call. George resumed talking with her mother, telling her about the fake message they had received.

"Why, how dreadful!" exclaimed Mrs. Fayne.

"It's wicked," said George. "Nancy has almost solved the mystery. The furniture thief is here. It was a pretty cruel method for him to use to get Nancy out of this area."

Mrs. Fayne felt that in view of what had happened, Nancy should not pursue the case any longer.

"Mother, you know how Nancy is," George replied. "She won't give up!"

"I suppose not," George's mother replied. "But do tell her to be careful, and you and Bess watch your step too."

George promised to do so, then hung up. Nancy came down the stairs and hugged George. She complimented the quick-witted girl for realizing the call might be a fake.

"Mrs. Roger Hoelt got the better of me that time," she said ruefully.

Nancy and the other girls, weary from their long day and the fright they had just had, went to bed early. All of them wanted to be fresh for the exciting detective work ahead of them.

The following morning, the girls were downstairs even before Mrs. Glick appeared. Not knowing what she had planned for breakfast, they walked outside. Henner was practicing nearby with his slingshot.

"Whom are you shooting now?" George asked him playfully.

"Goliath," the little boy answered. "I'm David."

The girls laughed, but Henner did not. He said he was perfecting his aim so that if any bad people came around to bother Nancy, he could use his slingshot as David had.

"Oh, Henner, you mustn't have such ideas," Nancy said. "If any bad people come around here, you let your dad handle them."

Henner was not convinced. He insisted that he was bigger than Nancy realized and was old enough to help if anything like that should happen. Nancy said no more on the subject. Deciding to pick some flowers for the breakfast table, she wandered off to the garden.

She had just gathered a large bouquet when suddenly she heard Bess shriek, "Look out!"

Nancy started to turn to find out what Bess meant. She was too late. At that moment something hit her in the back of the neck and she slumped to the ground, unconscious.

Bess was at her friend's side almost immediately. "Oh, Nancy!" she wailed.

Behind her, Henner was saying, "I didn't mean to do it. Is Nancy bad hurt?" The little boy dashed over to the girls.

By this time, George had also run up and together she and Bess carried Nancy into the house and laid her on a sofa. Mrs. Glick, who was just coming downstairs, rushed to find out what had happened.

"I did it, Mama!" Henner cried. "Oh, Mama, maybe I've killed Nancy with my slingshot."

Before his startled mother could calm the small boy, Henner hurried up the stairs, weeping. Mrs. Glick immediately turned her attention to Nancy.

"This is dreadful," the woman said.

She inquired where Nancy had been hit with the stone, and upon learning it was in the back of the neck, said at once, "We must quick get the doctor!" She made the call, then returned to Nancy. She took hold of one of the girl's hands and began to murmur a prayer. Bess, meanwhile, had wrung out a cloth in cold water, which she now placed on Nancy's forehead. George began chafing her friend's wrists.

Nancy slowly regained consciousness but was still groggy when the doctor arrived twenty minutes later. He said that, fortunately, Nancy had received only a glancing blow, judging by the scratches on the back of her neck. The doctor assured her friends that she would be all right, but should be quiet the rest of the day.

When Nancy's mind cleared, she smiled wanly and asked what had happened to her. George related the details of the accident.

Henner, meanwhile, had quietly come downstairs. "Poor Henner!" Nancy remarked. "Please don't punish him, Mrs. Glick. He meant no harm."

Mrs. Glick said she felt sure her son had learned his lesson but that she would take away the boy's slingshot. A few minutes later the doctor said he was sure Nancy would suffer no ill effects from the accident and that he must be going.

"I want you to rest today, Miss Drew. Don't even walk around—stay on this sofa until bedtime," he ordered.

He left at once, giving Nancy no opportunity to object. When she sadly mentioned having to postpone her sleuthing, Bess spoke up.

"Finding Roger Hoelt isn't worth risking your health," she said sternly. "Nancy, if you try to get off that sofa, I'm going to tie you down."

Nancy smiled. At the moment she entertained no such thought. Going to sleep was the only thing that appealed to her. For the rest of the day, Nancy napped a good bit and ate lightly. She went to bed right after dusk. To her own and everyone else's relief, she felt fine the next morning and ready to resume the search for Manda and her thieving employers, the Hoelts.

As soon as breakfast was over, Mrs. Glick playfully shooed the girls out of the house. They headed for the convertible. To their surprise, the car was not in its usual place by the barn.

"Did one of you move it yesterday?" Nancy asked.

The cousins shook their heads. "Maybe Mr. Glick put the car in the barn," George suggested. But he had not.

Then the girls went to the little stone building near the barn, where Mr. Glick had his cobbler's shop. They asked the kindly man where the convertible was.

"I, too, have wondered," he replied, "but I thought one of you girls had moved it."

Nancy, Bess, and George frantically searched everywhere, but the convertible was nowhere on the Glick farm.

"It's been stolen!" Bess cried out.

CHAPTER XVII

Wheel Off!

THE full import of Bess's words dawned on Nancy and George. There was no doubt, they realized with despair, that Nancy's convertible had been stolen!

"You've been hexed again," Bess added dolefully.

"Whether it was a hex or not, it's certainly bad luck," Nancy agreed. "I'll bet Roger Hoelt is responsible for this. He couldn't get me to leave this area, so he thought of another trick. Without a car it will be more difficult for us to find his hideout."

"But that isn't going to stop you, is it?" George asked at once.

"Of course not!" Nancy said, tossing her head vehemently. "It gives me an even better reason for finding him. I'm sure my car is at the Hoelt hideout."

"Why not rent another one?" Bess suggested.

Nancy said it was an excellent suggestion, but first she would notify the police. It was possible that the car thief was not Roger Hoelt but a local prankster. If so, the police might easily locate the convertible. It might even have been abandoned on some nearby road.

By now, all the Glicks had assembled and were aghast to hear the story. Henner felt particularly bad that Nancy was having more trouble. He shyly took one of her hands in his own.

"Nancy," he said, "to make up for what I did yesterday I want to help you now."

The little boy had such a pleading look in his eyes that Nancy gave him a loving hug. "I'll try to figure out how you can assist me," she replied.

Henner said he already had an idea. His face brightened as he said it was not too far to the *schnitz*. "I'll drive you there with our horse and carriage," he said.

"That might be a good solution," Nancy said, smiling. "But first I'll report the theft."

She hurried into the house and called State Police headquarters. Within half an hour an officer arrived and took down all the data. He also inspected the area where the car had been parked.

Presently the officer picked out a set of footprints intermingled with several others, which he declared were those of a man wearing shoes that were different from those of the Amish.

"Have you any idea of whom they might belong to?" the trooper asked Nancy.

She hesitated. "I can only guess," she replied. "I think to Roger Hoelt, whom you already know about. I suspect he's somewhere in this area and is trying to prevent me from locating him."

The officer said he would add this theft incident to the list of suspected charges against Roger Hoelt. As he stepped into his car, he promised to get in touch with Nancy as soon as he had a lead on her stolen convertible.

The family had breakfast. Afterward, Mrs. Glick said the girls were to do no more housework. "You have too much on your minds already," she stated firmly.

Nancy began to grow restless after another hour had passed by and no word had come from the State Police. Finally she said that with Mrs. Glick's approval, she would like to accept Henner's offer to drive her to the *schnitz* in the carriage.

"Of course," Mrs. Glick said. "And I shall also go with you. It may be dangerous and you should have an older person along. If Papa did not have to be so careful since his accident, I would ask him to go."

"I'll be there, ain't?" Henner exclaimed. "I'll protect everyone! I'm strong!"

His mother looked at him for several seconds,

apparently debating whether the boy was old enough to accompany them on what might be a hazardous mission. Finally she smiled. "You are getting to be a big boy. I believe you might help us. Yes, Henner, you may go."

Henner whooped with delight and dashed from the house to hitch up the horse. Within ten minutes he was calling to his passengers. Becky followed the group outside with a wistful expression. Her mother had already laid out some work for the girl to do.

"And besides," Mrs. Glick said, "you must fix a good lunch for Papa, Becky."

George and Bess got into the rear seat of the carriage. Henner took the reins, with his mother beside him and Nancy on the left end. They followed Groeszdawdi Esch's directions.

Soon they reached a side road that was full of ruts, and the carriage settled into a deep one. The horse plodded along at a snail's pace. About five-hundred yards farther on, the road took a sharp turn to the left.

Henner guided the horse around the corner, but in so doing forgot about the groove, which did not turn in their direction. The front wheels pulled out of the rut and settled into another pair of carriage tracks. The rear wheels remained in the former rut. At this instant a rabbit leaped in front of the horse. Frightened, the horse sprang up, giving the carriage such a hard jerk that the left wheel came off.

Mrs. Glick had helped her startled son rein in the horse by the time the carriage had settled in a tilted position on the road.

"So *druzzel!*" Mrs. Glick cried as everyone got out to survey the damage.

Henner, feeling he was again to blame, began to cry. His mother comfortingly said she doubted that the accident could have been avoided.

"But," Henner sputtered, "I was trying so hard to be helpful to Nancy. First I hurt her with my slingshot and now I cannot drive her to the *schnitz.* I am a failure, ain't?"

"Don't say that, Henner," Nancy said. "You have been most helpful to me and my friends since we have been here."

"You are not responsible for this mishap," his mother explained. "This is a dreadful road. Something should be done about it."

After examining the wheel, Mrs. Glick announced that it would be impossible for them to put it back on the carriage. It was a job for a wheelwright.

"What are we going to do?" Bess asked.

Mrs. Glick looked thoughtful for a few moments, then said that the Beiler farm was just across the fields. Turning to Nancy, she suggested that she and Henner ride the horse over there and try to borrow a carriage.

"Henner," his mother said, "you know Michael Beiler in school. I'm sure his family will help."

"*Ya*," replied the small boy, and began to unhitch the horse. When this was done, he and Nancy got on the animal's back and started off.

It was a mile's ride across the fields to the Beiler farm. Coming in sight of it, Nancy and Henner noticed many carriages and people around. Uprights for a new building were being put in place.

"It is a barn-raising," Henner explained. "Michael's papa had a bad fire and a barn burned down."

Then, proudly, Henner went on to say that in Amish country neighbors always helped one another to erect new buildings. "This way we are the money in," he said. "And a barn-raising is fun. Everybody gets a lot to eat."

There was a great bustle of activity in the Beiler barnyard. Some of the Amish farmers were bringing up lumber, others were lifting beams into place. In the short time since Nancy had first noticed the barn-raising from the fields, a great deal of construction had been done.

"It will be ready for the floor by dinnertime," said Henner, jumping to the ground.

Nancy also alighted from the horse and tried to get several different workers' attention. But everyone seemed to be too busy to tell her where she might find Mr. Beiler.

As she wondered where Mr. Beiler might be,

Nancy saw that Henner had spied Michael Beiler and had run up to see his playmate. Just then one of the workers cried out, *"Heist nus!"*

Nancy watched, fascinated, as several of the men began to hoist a heavy beam with their hands. But the next moment her interest changed to horror. The beam tipped, slipped from the men's grip, and began to fall directly toward Henner and Michael!

CHAPTER XVIII

Another Hex

WITH lightning speed Nancy dashed forward to Henner and Michael. Fortunately, the falling beam hit a crosspiece, which slowed its descent. The momentary delay gave Nancy a chance to push both boys out of the way and jump to safety herself.

The youngsters sprawled flat on the ground just as the beam crashed to the earth behind them. Bewildered, they scrambled up and looked around. Suddenly Henner realized that Nancy had saved their lives.

"Oh, Nancy," he cried out, "you kept us from being dead already yet!"

"Thank you! Thank you!" Michael exclaimed.

By this time, several of the workers had left their posts and rushed toward the three. In both English and Pennsylvania Dutch, they commended Nancy for her quick action.

One man separated himself from the group and stepped forward. "I am Mr. Beiler," he said. "I told my son not to come near the building. I thank you for saving him."

Mr. Beiler added that Nancy was no doubt a stranger in the neighborhood and asked her name. She gave it, then stated her reason for coming to the farm. Mr. Beiler replied that he would be very glad to lend her his carriage.

He promised that he and his sons would repair the broken carriage after the barn-raising was over, and return it to the Glicks the following day.

"You're very kind," said Nancy gratefully. "I don't want to interrupt the work here. Could Henner and Michael hitch up the horse?"

As they talked, Nancy noticed a woman coming toward them from the house. When she walked up, Mr. Beiler introduced his wife.

Tears came to the woman's eyes when she learned that Nancy had saved the lives of her youngest boy and of Henner Glick. Smiling at Nancy, she said, "You are a brave girl. Please let me show my appreciation. In the kitchen we are getting ready a big dinner to serve to the men. I want you and Henner to eat some of it."

Nancy thanked her and said she must hurry back to Mrs. Glick and the friends she had left on the road. But she did walk to the kitchen with Mrs. Beiler while the boys got the carriage.

Nancy had never seen so much food in one house! It seemed to her that there was enough to feed a small army. On the table were dishes piled high with the traditional "seven sweets and seven sours," which the Pennsylvania Dutch housewife serves at meals. At least fifty moon pies were on trays at one side of the kitchen, waiting to be baked. On the floor stood crocks of *fasnachts,* fried chicken, and pickle relish.

After casting her eye about and introducing several friends who were helping her, Mrs. Beiler picked up a large angel-food cake with whipped-cream frosting.

"Please take this," Mrs. Beiler requested. "I will wrap it for you."

She also insisted upon giving Nancy several pieces of fried chicken, a dozen doughnuts, and a jug of lemonade. At this moment Henner drove up to the door and the food was lifted into the carriage. Nancy thanked Mrs. Beiler once more, then climbed into the wagon, and the young driver turned toward the field over which they had come.

When he and Nancy reached the others, who were beginning to worry, Henner immediately told them about the falling beam. His mother's eyes opened wide and she put an arm around Nancy's shoulders. With a catch in her voice, she said, "I must admit that I never thought any women were so brave as the Amish. But you have made me see that a girl does not have to be brought up like a pioneer to be courageous and helpful to others."

Nancy flushed at the compliment. Then she showed the food Mrs. Beiler had sent and everyone stared in astonishment at the huge quantities. Bess insisted that they take time out to eat, and no one else had to be persuaded. All of it was as delicious as it looked, especially the cake, which Mrs. Glick declared must contain two dozen eggs!

"And the beating of them surely took an hour," she added.

As soon as they finished eating, they started off once more. This time Mrs. Glick, an experienced driver, took the reins. They kept to the field, crossing several narrow roads. Finally Nancy said that according to Groeszdawdi Esch's directions, they were nearing the old Hoelt farm where the *schnitz* was.

"Do you think we should leave the horse and buggy and walk the rest of the way?" Mrs. Glick asked Nancy.

After a moment's thought Nancy said that if Roger Hoelt were on the property he probably had it guarded and already knew they were coming. "I doubt that it would do any good to try hiding the horse and carriage," she said. "And if he isn't there, it will be better to have them with us. We may as well drive right up to the place."

They went on. Skirting a small woods, the searchers suddenly came upon a long, low, dilapidated wooden building. Mrs. Glick reined in the horse and stopped.

"This must be the old apple storehouse," she commented.

The others gazed at it. There was no sign of activity around the building, but they had an uneasy feeling that someone might be hiding inside. They all wondered if this was the place where the stolen furniture was stored.

"We'll start our search," Nancy announced. "I suggest that we divide forces. Bess and George, suppose you go in one direction and the Glicks and I will take another."

Bess did not like to see the group split up, but finally agreed that it was the most practical plan.

"But not until we all go into that storehouse together and look around," she said firmly.

Nancy led the way. She pushed open a creaky door and the group entered the lower floor of the two-story building. Through the cracks between the wide boards enough sunlight filtered in so that they could plainly see the interior. There was one large room—completely empty!

Cautiously, Nancy and her friends climbed to the second floor. The situation here was the same. To convince herself that there were no secret closets or other hiding places, the young detective made a thorough search but she found nothing.

"There must be a house and barns on the property," she said. "Let's find them."

Outside, the group separated. Bess and George cautiously made their way along the edge of the woods, planning to skirt it completely. Nancy, Mrs. Glick, and Henner decided to drive the carriage across the clearing and along a lane that ran through the woods.

At the far end of the woods they came to the dooryard of the farmhouse. As the three alighted from the carriage, Henner suddenly cried out with fright and pointed.

Ahead of them was a witch tree! And painted on it was half of the now-familiar hex sign!

"Look!" Henner shrieked.

A hand holding a paintbrush was just reaching around the tree. No other part of a human body was visible. The watchers stared in astonishment at the weird sight.

Henner clung to his mother's skirts. Mrs. Glick looked grim, and Nancy's spine tingled. For a brief second she felt as if she were seeing a ghostly apparition. Then she brushed this thought aside and dashed forward to see who was behind the tree.

Fully expecting the person to be Roger Hoelt, she was amazed to find a stout, dull-looking boy, about sixteen years old. He stared at the girl stupidly.

"Look!" Henner shrieked.

"What are you doing?" she cried. "And who lives here?"

The youth continued to gawk at her and did not answer. Mrs. Glick, who had run up, began to question him in Pennsylvania Dutch. But he did not utter a word and looked as if he failed to comprehend what she was saying.

Suddenly Nancy had an idea. Perhaps the boy was a deaf mute! She decided to test him.

While Mrs. Glick was trying to get the boy to talk, Nancy quickly kicked a large stone toward the tree. It made a loud noise when it hit the trunk, but the boy paid no attention. Now she was sure he could not hear and apparently could not speak.

"I wonder if he works for Roger Hoelt," Nancy mused aloud.

"He probably does," Mrs. Glick said. "Do you think we ought to tie him up in the carriage until our search is over? If we don't, I'm afraid he may run off and warn the man."

Nancy wondered about this. She said that her chief concern now was to find Manda Kreutz and induce her to leave the Hoelts' before Nancy notified the police.

"Then we won't worry about this boy," said Mrs. Glick. "Where do we go next?"

Before Nancy could make up her mind, she heard Bess calling her. "Come quickly!" the girl urged.

"Where are you?" Nancy called back.

"In the woods near the house," Bess replied. Nancy dashed in the direction of Bess's voice, requesting that the Glicks watch the strange boy. When Nancy reached her friends she could hardly believe her eyes. Talking to George and Bess was a sweet-faced Amish girl—Manda Kreutz!

CHAPTER XIX

Caught!

"Manda!" Nancy cried excitedly, running up to the Amish girl. "I'm so glad we've found you at last! Are you all right?"

"Yes," replied Manda, looking a little surprised. She went on to say that she was living with Mr. and Mrs. Roger Hoelt. "They are very nice people and are restoring this old house."

"Nice people!" George cried. "They're anything but that!"

Manda frowned, then asked George what she meant by this.

"You explain, Nancy," George said. "Bess and I haven't told Manda anything about the mystery."

After hearing the story, Manda was amazed. She could not believe it. The Hoelts had been very kind to her and were paying her good wages.

Manda added that they were Church Amish from
Ohio and spoke Pennsylvania Dutch very well.

"I do not see how Mr. Hoelt could be a thief,"
she said stubbornly.

"Well, he is," George told her bluntly. "And
the sooner you get out of here the better."

Sadly Manda hung her head, saying she had
no place else to go. Her papa would not let her
return home, and she did not want to work in
Lancaster.

Nancy smiled. "I've talked with your mother
and father, Manda. They want you to come home.
Your father regrets being so harsh and will be
glad to have you back."

The Amish girl looked at Nancy as if this were
not possible. Finally she said, "You speak the
truth?"

Bess looked indignant. "Of course Nancy's telling the truth."

But Nancy did not blame Manda for not being
completely persuaded, either that her family
wanted her back or that Roger Hoelt was a thief.
"I must convince her," Nancy thought. Aloud
she said, "Manda, have the Hoelts moved any
furniture into the house?"

"Oh, yes."

"Beautiful antique furniture?" Nancy asked.
"Are there one or more tables from George Washington's home?"

Manda looked startled. "You know this?"

Nancy gave her additional details of the mystery, and finally the Amish girl said she believed now that Mr. Hoelt was indeed a thief. She would leave the Hoelts' employ immediately. But she did not want to report them to the police.

"You will have to do that," she said to the young sleuth.

Suddenly Nancy recalled the boy who had been painting the hex sign on the witch tree and asked Manda who he was.

"He is a harmless boy who cannot hear or speak," the Amish girl answered. "Todd lives here too. Mr. Hoelt writes out everything for him to do. Todd is not very smart, but he is a good worker."

"Did Mr. Hoelt ask him to paint the symbol on the tree?" Nancy queried, telling of the strange way in which it was being done.

Manda nodded. Mr. Hoelt had claimed it was a hex sign used by his family years before. He was very proud of it, and planned to have the hex sign painted on the barn and various other places when he restored the farm.

"He told Todd to paint the symbol on a tree but not to let anyone see him." Manda laughed. "The poor boy probably hid when he saw you coming but tried to go on with the painting."

The girls smiled, then Nancy asked Manda how she had located the farm. The Amish girl revealed that Mr. Hoelt had not given her very clear directions when he had suggested she come to work for them.

"All he said was that the house was near the old *schnitz*. I could find it by looking for two witch trees."

"Is there really such a thing as a witch tree?" Bess asked. "We thought it was just a nickname for a tree with witches' broom growing on it."

"That is right," Manda replied. "I figured Mr. Hoelt meant an old tree with *hex bayse* near the *schnitz*. I asked lots of people where the *schnitz* was, but nobody seemed to know. Then I met an old man on the road and he told me to come here. When I saw the witch trees, I knew this was the right place."

Suddenly Manda looked around her, a frightened expression coming over her face. She said all of them should leave at once.

"You mean before Mr. and Mrs. Hoelt catch us?" George put in.

"Not exactly," Manda replied. "But they will be back this evening. I want to be far away when they drive in."

The fact that the Hoelts were not at home pleased Nancy. This would give her a chance to make a positive identification of the furniture before reporting the Hoelts to the police.

"Please show us first where the antiques are," Nancy requested.

"All right. But we must hurry," Manda said, starting for the house.

Nancy walked beside her and asked the girl if she had ever heard of an old secret connected with the farm. Manda shook her head.

Nancy pursued the subject. "Manda, did you overhear the Hoelts say anything about a mystery connected with the place?"

Again Manda said no. Then Nancy asked her if she had screamed while running in the woods near one of the smaller houses on the property.

Manda smiled. "Oh, that was Mrs. Hoelt," she replied. "She saw a stray dog."

Manda was amazed to learn that the three girls had been so close to the farm such a short time before. When Nancy told her about the attic episode, Manda said this would account for Mr. Hoelt's coming into the house with his hair and clothes very dirty. He had said that he had been in the attic of a relative's house, looking for an old family Bible he had heard about the day before.

The Amish girl opened the rear door of the farmhouse. In the kitchen were just a few pots, pans, and dishes. Manda explained that the Hoelts, had brought in only four cots and the antique furniture, since they planned to redecorate the house completely. The antiques had been stored in two attic storage rooms, because the painters would soon start work.

"Mr. Hoelt told me never to mention the fur-

niture because someone might try to steal it,"
Manda explained.

George said in disgust, "A clever cover-up."

"Shall we go upstairs now?" Manda asked.

"Yes," said Nancy. "I have a list with me of
the furniture stolen from the Follett mansion in
River Heights. I'll see if the pieces here appear to
be the same ones."

The four girls climbed two flights of stairs to
the attic. Here there was a center hall with a window in the rear. A storage room opened off each
side of the hall. Nancy noted the heavy Dutch
doors, which had unusual locks. They were made
of iron and were fully six inches square. An
enormous key protruded from each lock, each key
with a loop on the end that was as big around as
any of Nancy's bracelets.

Manda unlocked one of the doors. In the light
from the hallway and from a small ventilator at
the far end of the room, the girls could see several pieces of old furniture.

Nancy went from one to another, eying them
carefully. After looking them all over, she said,
"I'm sure these pieces came from Mrs. Follett's
home. But, Manda, none of the George Washington tables is here."

"They are across the hall," the girl replied.
"Mr. Hoelt said they were the most valuable and
put the tables by themselves."

She unlocked the other storage room and the

girls went inside. There were four George Washington tables! Nancy surmised that two were genuine, while the other two were the copies Mr. Zinn had made. So Roger Hoelt had found the valuable matching cherry table!

Nancy asked Manda if she knew where it had come from. "Mr. Hoelt said he bought it in a New York antique shop."

"Well," she said, smiling, "our search is ended."

"I'm glad," Bess sighed. "You deserve a lot of credit, Nance, but it will be a relief to wind up this case."

"And I vote for that too," said George, "although it has been a lot of fun. Congratulations, Nancy."

"I never could have done it alone," the young detective spoke up quickly.

Manda thought it was marvelous that Nancy had traced the stolen pieces. "And to think also that you fixed everything for me with Papa and Mama so I can go home. It would be wonderful to go now, ain't?"

"We'll start right away," said Nancy. "And we'll stop at the nearest farm with a telephone and call the police. They should be here to greet Mr. and Mrs. Hoelt when they arrive."

The girls were so absorbed in their discussion that no one but Nancy, out of the corner of her eye, saw the shadow that suddenly fell across the doorway. Whirling around, she caught a fleeting glimpse of a man who thundered, "You will never do that! You will die first!"

With this, he slammed the door and locked it!

"Mr. Hoelt!" Manda cried. "Let us out!" The reply was a mocking laugh from the other side of the barrier.

The girls leaped toward the door, pounding on it and trying to batter it down. At the top of her voice Manda yelled that Mr. Hoelt had no right to lock her in. He must release all of them at once!

Her plea went unheeded. Then the girls heard Roger Hoelt hurrying down the stairway.

"We must get out and capture that thief!" Nancy cried with determination.

Together, the girls threw their weight against the door time after time, trying to break it down. Their efforts were futile.

"We're prisoners!" Bess wailed. "He's going to leave us here to die!"

CHAPTER XX

SOS

FRANTIC that they would suffocate in the hot, stuffy attic, the four girls continued their efforts to break down the locked door. But finally, their shoulders bruised and sore, they were forced to give up.

Bess was on the verge of tears. In the darkness the others could hear her moan softly. "Nobody will ever find us here."

Nancy felt far from cheerful, but she tried to encourage her friends by saying that perhaps Mrs. Glick and Henner would bring help.

"Oh no they won't!" Bess wailed. "That awful man has probably captured them too by this time!"

Manda had not uttered a word and Nancy asked her how she felt. "I am all right," the Amish girl said. "But it is my fault that all of us are trapped here. I should have known Mr. Hoelt might return earlier, even though he told me evening. He rarely went anywhere in the daytime. He was always out at night."

Nancy persuaded the girl that she was not to blame. But the young detective also felt bad because she had been so close to capturing the thief, and then had lost her chance.

George, practical as usual, pushed one of the tables to the wall directly under the ventilator. She climbed up to breathe in some fresh air and to investigate the ventilator as a means of escape. The bars were tightly built into the wall with three-inch spaces between them.

"No chance to get out this way," she said, "but if anybody feels faint, I suggest that you come up here for a little air."

"Maybe we can use the ventilator for another purpose," said Nancy. "We can signal for help."

"With what?" Bess asked forlornly.

Manda remembered having seen a kerosene lantern in the room. "Is that what you had in mind, Nancy, using a light to signal with?"

"Yes, Manda. You're becoming a good detective."

The Amish girl found the lantern, then asked if anyone had a match. Nancy produced a packet from her dress pocket. Matches and a flashlight were part of her detective equipment, but this time the flashlight was in her stolen car. She lighted a match and Manda tested the lamp.

"It's all right and there's enough oil in it," the Amish girl stated.

"It won't do any good to signal until it's dark " Bess spoke up. "And by that time there's no telling what may happen to us."

To pass the time, Nancy decided to try locating the secret drawers in the Washington tables. As she worked, Nancy told Manda the story. But after a half hour's search Nancy had not found the drawers.

"They're certainly well concealed," she said. Bess and George took turns but had no better luck. Suddenly Nancy had a new idea. If the secret drawers were so hard to find, it was possible that the gypsy woman had not known about them. If she had secreted a note in one of the tables, it might well be in some other part of it.

Nancy examined every inch of the two tables. Finally it occurred to her that one of the legs looked just a trifle different in length. When she measured it against the other three, using her skirt as a ruler, she found the leg to be about one-sixteenth of an inch longer than the others.

Standing the table on its side, she began to wiggle the leg. After several tries she felt it loosen slightly. Excited, Nancy twisted the leg and found that it actually unscrewed. In a moment she had it off.

Wedged inside was a small piece of paper!

By this time, the other girls had jumped to her

side. As they watched in astonishment Nancy removed the note and read it. George held the lantern.

> *Emil, My Beloved,*
>
> *Someday our paths will cross again, but now I must flee. Wherever I am, my love and thoughts will always be for you.*
>
> *Before I leave, I want to warn you. Yesterday I learned the secret of your farm. I nearly stumbled into a deep hole located near a stand of oak trees—you know the place, for we have often met there. Had I been alone, I would have vanished like members of your family.*
>
> *But my brother Gato rescued me. We wondered about the hole. He went down on a rope with a lantern and found a crystal cave. It is large and beautiful and someday will bring you riches.*
>
> *I have planted bushes of wild flowers from the forest over the hole, so you will never fall in. This will prove my love for you. I beg you to leave your papa and find me.*
>
> *Your loving gypsy,*
> *Amaya*

Speechless, the girls read and reread the note. At last they knew the secret of the Hoelt farm!

"Roger Hoelt will return here someday and find this," Bess said dejectedly. "He will be a rich man and all of us will be dead!"

George chided her cousin for such melancholy thoughts. "We'll signal and get out of here yet!" she said with determination.

Fortunately, dusk came early. Nancy climbed to the table top and held the lantern up to the ventilator. Passing one hand in front of the light at intervals, she gave the SOS signal. Over and over she repeated this until her arms were weary. George climbed up to relieve her, then Bess. They all knew the call. Manda marveled at such efficiency.

"I hope someone sees it soon and understands," she said.

At this moment, the girls heard heavy footsteps on the attic steps and caught their breath. Was Roger Hoelt returning with reinforcements? Would the girls be further harmed? Would he now be the possessor of the secret in the table and take advantage of it?

The key turned in the door. The girls stood together, ready to defend themselves. The door opened. To their relief, they saw two police officers—Wagner and Schmidt.

"Oh, boy!" George cried out. "I never was more glad in my whole life to see anybody!"

"Were you giving an SOS signal?" Officer Wagner asked.

"Yes," said Nancy, and she quickly told the police how they had been imprisoned by Hoelt.

Then she showed the policemen the note about the crystal cave.

"I can hardly believe all this!" said Officer Wagner. "Nancy Drew, it is remarkable how you have solved this mystery."

"But it isn't completely solved," the girl detective replied. "We still have to find Mr. and Mrs. Hoelt." She said that possibly they were in her car, which had been stolen.

"A very good deduction," Officer Schmidt said. "We haven't received word that your convertible was picked up."

As the whole group hurried down the stairs and went outdoors, Nancy asked the policemen if they had seen Mrs. Glick and her son Henner.

"No," Officer Wagner answered. "Are they here too?"

"I don't know," said Nancy, explaining that the Glicks had come to the *schnitz* with the girls but had stayed behind near the witch tree.

"They may be prisoners," she said. "We'd better go there and look."

They hurried along with the policemen, who beamed their bright flashlights ahead. As they approached the witch tree, the rays of light picked out the woman and her son, gagged and bound to the tree trunk.

The two were quickly released; then stories were exchanged. Mrs. Glick said that when Nancy had gone off she and Henner had stayed behind to watch the deaf-mute boy so he could make no trouble.

"But he got away just before Mr. and Mrs. Hoelt drove in with Nancy's car," Mrs. Glick went on. "We tried to escape, but they caught us. They had another man with them."

"I'll report all of this at once," said Officer Wagner. Over his shortwave car radio, he sent a message to headquarters, giving a full report and requesting that every road be covered until Mr. and Mrs. Hoelt and their companion were apprehended. Then he added, "We'll drive Nancy Drew and her friends home before we return."

Mrs. Glick wanted to take the horse and buggy, but the officer suggested that she leave them until morning. They all crowded into the officers' car, which was parked on one of the little-used roads.

It was a long and bumpy ride back to the Glicks'. On the way Nancy, who was sitting in front between the two officers, asked what had brought them to the old Hoelt homestead.

"You didn't just happen to be there to answer my signal," she said, a twinkle in her eye.

The officers confessed that they had been making a very intensive investigation of Roger Hoelt. They had learned about the family homestead and had decided to go there and look around.

"You were just in the nick of time," Bess said. "I was nearly suffocated."

Officer Wagner smiled. "I'm glad we found you, but that doesn't change the fact that it was Nancy Drew who solved this case."

Nancy made no comment. As always happened when she had solved a mystery, she began to wonder what the next challenge would be. It was not long in coming, for at that very moment events were taking place that would enmesh the young detective in another exciting adventure, *The Hidden Window Mystery*.

The police officers kept their radio tuned to headquarters during the entire drive. To everyone's elation, the news was flashed to them a little later that Mr. and Mrs. Hoelt and their accomplice had been arrested. They had been caught riding in Nancy's car, which would be returned to its owner at the Glick home.

The broadcast went on to say that Roger Hoelt had confessed to having posed as an Amish man from Ohio. In his childhood he had lived in Lancaster and so had learned the customs and language of these people. Therefore, it had been easy for him to pose as one of them.

Hoelt admitted that when Nancy found out he had taken the Follett furniture he had tried in every way to keep her from locating him. He had resorted both to violence and to defamation of her character.

"The witch tree symbol was his undoing," the police officer announced on the shortwave radio.

Hoelt had copied his family's old hex sign on a piece of paper and lost it at the Follett home when he stole the furniture. When he came back to look for it, Nancy and Mrs. Tenney surprised him there and he had fled to the second floor. Hearing of Nancy's plan to search the house, he had run away and checked out of the hotel. Three days before that, he had made a phone call to his accomplice in Lancaster, saying he was ready for the man to bring his truck and steal the antique furniture.

The evening of the day when Nancy had surprised him in the Follett mansion, Hoelt had planned to spy on the Drew home. While cruising back and forth in his car, he had seen a chance to hit Togo and had done so out of spite.

Later that evening he had phoned Mrs. Tenney. Disguising his voice, he had posed as an antique dealer from New York and had cleverly induced Mrs. Tenney to tell him all she knew about Nancy's part in the case, including the fact that she was going to Lancaster to try to find the thief. Hearing this, Hoelt had at once started for Lancaster. On the way he had mailed the warning letter in Montville.

On a trip back to Lancaster, after his release from prison, Hoelt had heard about the secret in the old table. Since the secret was reputed to have some connection with the old Hoelt property, he had seen a chance to find a treasure, acquire the property cheap, and then become wealthy.

From the time he had learned Nancy had taken the case, he had worked against her, trying to keep her from locating him.

"But he failed!" cried Manda, leaning forward to hug Nancy. "If you had not come to Amish country, I would not now be going home to my parents. Oh, I am so happy to have met a wonderful person like you!"

Nancy smiled and returned the compliment as Manda dropped her voice confidently. "I will tell you three girls a secret," she said. "I met a fine young man in Lancaster who wants to marry me in a month. Papa and Mama will like him, too, and I know they will give me a big wedding. Nancy, George, and Bess—you will promise to come, please?"

"We'd love to!" exclaimed Nancy, as George said, "You couldn't keep us away."

"It sounds dreamy!" Bess said with delight. "And you Amish have wonderful wedding feasts." She chuckled. "Ain't?"

Match Wits with The Hardy Boys®!

Collect the Complete
Hardy Boys Mystery Stories®
by Franklin W. Dixon

Celebrate over 70 Years with the World's Greatest Super Sleuths!

Match Wits with Super Sleuth Nancy Drew!

Collect the Complete
Nancy Drew Mystery Stories®
by Carolyn Keene

Nancy Drew Back-to-Back

Celebrate over 70 years with the World's Best Detective